The Ties That Bind

Samantha Baca

Haven Brook Series

'Til Death Do Us Part

The Cradle Will Fall

The Ties That Bind

A Very Haven Christmas

Three Strikes, You're Gone

Contents

One	1
Two	7
Three	11
Four	17
Five	25
Six	29
Seven	33
Eight	41
Nine	49
Ten	55
Eleven	61
Twelve	69
Thirteen	79
Fourteen	83
Fifteen	89
Sixteen	97
Seventeen	105
Eighteen	111
Nineteen	121
Twenty	135
Twenty One	147
Twenty Two	159
Twenty Three	167
Twenty Four	171
Twenty Five	179
Twenty Six	185
Twenty Seven	187
Twenty Eight	191
Epilogue	199
Other Books By Samatha	205
Acknowledgements	207
About the Author	209

To my Nana Fay,
I'm sending a copy to heaven for you...

One
Grant

The snow was coming down heavy, making it nearly impossible to see more than a couple of feet ahead. I turned my high beams on, knowing that the likelihood of anyone else being out at this time of night during the worst storm Haven Brook had seen in twenty years was unlikely. Hell, I didn't want to be out in it myself. My gloved hand gripped the steering wheel as I slowed down to go through the curve I knew was coming.

Out of nowhere, a pair of headlights blinded me as I rounded the bend. I carefully tried to maneuver the truck to the side to avoid the other car, feeling the exact moment that I hit a patch of ice that sent the truck spinning. There was a loud noise as metal plowed into something solid. A horn blared, cutting into the calm silence of the night.

A few seconds later the truck came to a stop on the side of the hill, the tail end butted up against a thick tree. I put it in park and turned off the engine before I grabbed a flashlight out of the glove box and hopped out. It was pitch black which limited my visibility, even with a flashlight. I stepped carefully as the snow sunk around me with each step, patches of ice just inches below. Luckily, I knew the area and even though I was only in ankle deep snow now, it could be waist high in a matter of minutes.

I made my way toward the side of the road, making sure to stay alert for any oncoming traffic. The sound of the horn was getting closer as I walked toward a clearing on the other side of the two-lane highway. Plunged head first into an embankment of trees was the red sedan that had almost hit me. I quickly scanned the area with the flashlight as I made my way over, looking for anyone that might have been ejected from the vehicle.

I walked over to the driver's side window and looked in. A woman was face down against the airbag that had been deployed. I quickly moved the flashlight around and glanced in the backseat where I saw a little girl, not much older than my son, sitting in the backseat, crying. My heart raced as I tried to pull the door handle to open it, only to find the doors were locked.

"Can you unlock your door?" I screamed, hoping the little girl could hear me over the horn as I pointed to the lock. She shook her head no as she tried to open it. I let out a frustrated breath as I realized the child lock was probably on since I do the same thing for Liam. I smiled warmly at the girl and hoped that she could see it before I went back to the driver's side door. I knocked loudly on the glass, hoping the woman would come to so I wouldn't have to break it and scare the child.

A few seconds later she slowly lifted her head and looked around as she blinked a few times. Her eyes immediately went to the rearview mirror and I could see her lips move as she talked to the girl. I knocked again on the window, watching as she turned to look at me.

"Can you unlock the doors?" I shouted again, shivering as the wind whipped past me, leaving an icy chill in its place.

She nodded yes and pressed the button. I was relieved when I heard the sound and quickly reached forward to open the door. I had plenty of questions to ask her, including what the hell she was doing out in this weather with a child, but needed to get away from the blaring horn before I completely lost my hearing.

I gave her a few seconds after I opened the door so I didn't startle or overwhelm her. She looked like she was pretty out of it and from the way the front end of her car was wrapped around the tree, I could see why.

"My name is Grant, I'm going to help you guys out of the car and get you into my truck. Can you move?" I asked loudly as I looked between both of them before setting the flashlight on the hood of the car, casting enough light around them without blinding anyone.

"I can move, I'm not hurt," the little girl called back to me as she clutched a stuffed animal against her chest. She was still buckled in which made me hopeful that she didn't have any serious injuries.

"How about you, ma'am? Can you move? Are you hurt?" I looked directly at the woman as I scanned her body to check for any bleeding or signs of injuries.

"I can move, I think." She reached down and pushed the button to release her seatbelt. I grabbed the strap and pushed it to the side when it refused to wind back in place. She turned to look at me, still dazed as if she didn't know what to do.

"Very slowly, I want you to turn to the side and bring your legs out." I glanced around us, checking to make sure everything was still safe before asking them to get out. She nodded as she did what I asked and sat there waiting for me to continue.

"That's great," I said gently. "Now I'm going to reach in and I want you to grab onto my arm with both hands while I help you out. Are you ready?"

She nodded yes and slowly grabbed onto my arm, lifting herself out of the car as I brought my other arm behind to help steady her. She was a little wobbly at first but seemed to regain her balance fairly quickly. When I was confident that she wasn't going to fall, I turned my attention to the little girl.

"Okay honey, now it's your turn. Can you unbuckle your seatbelt while I unlock the door?" She smiled and pressed the button to release it as I heard the door unlock. I was thankful to see that her seatbelt immediately pulled back in and didn't appear to have been damaged in the accident. I opened the door and she scooted forward, taking my hand as she carefully stepped out of the car.

"Watch your step, it's very slick out here," I warned as I held her steady before helping to move her next to the woman.

"My truck is on the other side of the road, not too far away. Do you need anything from the car before we go?"

The woman looked dazed as she stared blankly at me. I ran a hand down the scruff on my face, knowing that we needed to get moving. I grabbed the flashlight from the hood and quickly scanned the car. Aside from a travel pillow and a few duffle bags, there wasn't much in there.

"We don't have anything, just those bags in the backseat. My mom has her purse and her phone up front in the passenger seat," the little girl offered as she shivered. I nodded as I reached in and grabbed the two duffle bags and slung them over my shoulder before walking around to the passenger side of the car. The door was hard to open from the damage of the accident but after a couple of hard pulls, I was able to pry it open enough to get inside. I grabbed the purse and cellphone from the seat and let the door slam shut. I stuffed the phone into my pocket and wrapped the purse over my shoulder along with the duffle bags before getting the flashlight situated.

I walked back around to the driver's side and stood next to them so they could hear me over the horn that was still blaring.

"We need to walk across the highway and over to the other side, do you think you guys can do that?"

I prayed they could, otherwise, this was going to take even longer if I had to carry both of them to the truck in separate trips. They both nodded and the little girl reached up and grabbed the woman's hand, forcing her out of her daze.

"Come on, mom, we need to walk across the street to get to the truck." Her voice was small but there was the maturity of a little girl who had to grow up way too quickly. It hit a little too close to home when I thought of Liam and how he grew up faster than he should have after his mom died.

The woman smiled and nodded before turning her head to look at me. The flashlight caught her features just right, casting a warm glow on her golden-brown hair. She was incredibly gorgeous, even with trickles of blood-stained on her head. I shook my head and forced myself to focus as I glanced toward the highway. It was one thing to get myself across an icy, snow-packed highway, knowing how to walk in this weather. It was another to get a woman and a child across safely, assuming that they didn't know how to walk in it given that they were severely underdressed for the weather to begin with.

"Alright, we better get going," I huffed as I drew in a cold breath of air. "What's your name, sweetie?" I asked, looking down at the little girl who was still holding the woman's hand.

"I'm Annie, this is my mom, Lacey." She looked up at her nervously, the way a child does when they get in trouble for giving too much information to a stranger.

"That's a pretty name." I smiled to try to put them both at ease. "Okay, we're going to walk very carefully up this small hill and onto the freeway. The snow has started to pack which will help keep us from having to walk on ice, but that doesn't mean that you won't still hit a patch. I want you to be very careful and take one step at a time. Make sure your foot is planted and secure before taking the next step, okay?"

They both nodded and slowly started walking toward me. We walked alongside each other and I was relieved that it was going faster than I thought. We reached the highway, which was empty, and made it across quickly without any problems. I could see the truck not too far off in the distance and was happy that we could finally get inside and warm up. I clicked the button to unlock the doors as we got closer. I shined the light toward the back, making sure there wasn't any damage that would keep us from getting out of there. More snow had fallen and had already covered up the footprints from where I had been earlier which meant that the storm was coming quickly and we needed to get moving before we were stranded for the night.

I opened the back door and helped Annie get in, making sure she was buckled in before reaching under the seat and pulling out a couple of blankets. I handed one to her as she smiled and grabbed it, quickly wrapping it tightly around herself as she shivered. I sat the duffle bags on the floor below the seat next to her and closed the door before walking around to the passenger door and helping Lacey inside. Once she was settled in, I handed her the other blanket and waited until she had pulled it around herself before putting on her seatbelt. I pulled the phone out of my pocket and handed it to her along with the purse before shutting the door and making my way around to climb in.

I stuck the key in the ignition and turned it, disappointed when it refused to start. I saw the look on Lacey's face from the corner of my eye as worry lines formed across her brow. I clenched my jaw and tried again, relieved when I heard it sputter a few times before it finally started. I made sure the four-wheel-drive was still turned on before slowly putting it in drive and easing up the side of the hill. Thank the Lord that it wasn't a steep hill. I couldn't deal with anything else tonight and was already frozen to the bone from being out in the cold for so long. I cranked up the heat and made sure the vents were aimed toward the back so Annie would get warm.

The drive back to my house wouldn't take long but I had no idea where they were planning to stay. If they hadn't made a reservation they were going to be screwed with everything already being booked for New Year's Eve. Haven Brook was far from a big city but they threw one of the best New Year's Eve parties and all of the neighboring small towns came in to celebrate which meant booming business for the two hotels that were still open.

"Where do you want me to take you?" I asked, keeping my eyes on the road to make sure there weren't any more close calls for the night.

"Um, if there's a hotel nearby, that would be great." Her voice was soft and had the loving tone that you would hear from a mother. It had been hard to hear her earlier with the horn blaring in my ears.

"Do you have a reservation?" I quickly glanced at her before focusing on the road again.

She shook her head no and looked out the window as she pulled the sleeve of her sweater over her hand and covered her mouth nervously.

"Okay, do you have anyone you could stay with?" I was trying to figure out what she was doing here in the first place, my mind completely boggled that she would attempt to drive through this storm without stopping to let it pass. This was just the beginning of it and according to the news, it was about to get really bad, really quick.

"I don't know anyone here, we were just passing through. I didn't expect for us to need to stay the night." Her tone changed slightly and I heard an edge to it.

I don't know what came over me but I looked in the rearview mirror into the eyes of a scared little girl and found myself doing the unthinkable.

"You can stay with me." I gripped the steering wheel tighter than necessary and stared at the road in front of me while trying to fight off the feelings of regret that were already starting to blossom.

Two
Lacey

I stared out the window into the darkness as the truck slowed down once we were in town. Subtly, I cast a glance at the stranger beside me, wondering what I was going to do with his offer for us to stay with him. I anxiously ran my tongue back and forth along the roof of my mouth as I tried to think through what options I had left.

My car was totaled, I was stuck in a small town with no place to stay, in the middle of a freaking blizzard. I shivered at the thought of what would have happened if he hadn't come to save us. Tears started to fill my eyes as I quickly blinked them away, pushing aside the images that had been haunting me for months. As much as I hated the thought of staying the night at some man's house that I didn't know, I hated the thought of what would happen if we didn't find somewhere to lay low for the night. I had no idea where I was but I could definitely tell that it was a small town, and you don't just show up in one and expect not to be the talk of it by morning.

I looked around as we turned left and started heading through a neighborhood of cozy-looking houses. Each one was slightly different than the other but overall they looked the same. A smile played across my lips as I imagined little kids playing in the street as their parents visited with the neighbors while they sat on the front porches drinking lemonade. That was always the life I thought I would have but it's funny the curveballs that were thrown at me instead.

A few minutes later the truck slowly eased into a driveway and I glanced back to see Annie had already fallen asleep. The truck crept forward as the garage door opened and I was thankful that I wouldn't have to try to carry her inside in the snow. The garage door closed quietly behind us as he turned off the engine and turned to smile at me.

He was a very attractive man, relatively clean-cut aside from the scruff on his face from missing a couple of days of shaving. In the dim light of the garage, I could see the slightest hint of blue in his eyes and had to reassure myself that serial killers were often good looking guys and not to let my guard down. Okay, so maybe I wasn't actually worried that he might be a serial killer. It was more likely that I was guarded because I couldn't remember the last time a man was genuinely nice to me without wanting something in return. I smiled back nervously as my fingers fumbled around, working to undo the seatbelt when he opened the door and got out, closing it softly behind him to keep from waking Annie. Once I had my seatbelt undone, I quietly opened the door, surprised to see him on the other side as he helped me out.

"Thanks, Gra—" I paused, completely embarrassed that I had already forgotten his name. I knew it started with a G but now that I was trying to use it, I couldn't remember it for the life of me. Was it Graham? Garth? Gonad? I wrinkled my nose and shook my head, knowing I must be delirious if I was considering that was his name.

I heard him chuckle as he tried to look away, a dimple making its way next to the smile that pulled across his face. He coughed to clear his laughter before looking back at me with a forced stoic expression on his face.

"I'm so sorry," I whispered as I felt the heat travel up my neck to my face. He let a small laugh out as he held up his hand to stop me from saying anything more.

"No worries, it's Grant," he laughed as he looked past me to the back seat. "Do you want me to carry her in for you?"

"Oh no, you don't have to do that. I'll get her, but thank you." I took a few steps back and quietly opened the door before reaching in and leaning across her to undo her seatbelt. Her puppy was clutched to her chest forcing a lump in my throat every time I saw how much she cherished the worn-out stuffed animal. I gently pulled it from her arms so I could pick her up, grabbing it once I had a good hold on her. I smiled as Grant turned and walked in front of me, opening the door as he stepped to the side to let me through.

I heard his footsteps beside me as he reached over and flipped on the light switch in the kitchen, casting enough light for us to see without it waking up Annie. The house already felt cozy and welcoming which was a nice feeling given everything that we had been through in the past 24 hours. He quickly showed me the kitchen and asked that we help ourselves to anything in the fridge before leading me around the corner into the living room. There was a long hallway that separated the two rooms with a staircase at the end.

I shifted my weight to try to adjust for Annie's weight when Grant noticed and pulled his brows together. The tour of the house wrapped up quickly as he cleared some books and a video game controller from the couch so I could set Annie down. He apologized several times, mostly muttering under his breath, about not having a spare room to offer us. The couch was big enough for Annie to sleep comfortably, and there was an oversized recliner in the corner that I could take. Honestly, I was happy to not have to sleep in the car as I had planned.

"This is perfect, thank you so much," I said quietly as I laid Annie down on the couch and pulled the blanket from the truck up over her. She looked so small and fragile while she was sleeping and I had to remind myself that she was only 8 and not the 14-year-old she sometimes acted like. She was growing up too fast, and unfortunately, life was forcing her to leave a part of her childhood behind with the hand she was dealt.

"I'll go grab your stuff from the truck and bring it in for you." His eyes shifted to Annie laying on the couch and I could see a look of concern on his face.

"Maybe we should get her to a hospital, have her checked out," he said warily with his hands on his hips. I looked down and looked at her as a flood of emotions swept over me as I had been wondering the same thing since we fled.

"She's fine, she just needs some rest." I swallowed hard and lifted my eyes, pinning him with a look that I hoped would shift his focus from her to me.

"You guys were in a pretty bad accident, you should go see a doctor and have them run tests."

"Trust me, I see this kind of stuff all the time. We're okay." I smiled the smile I was used to wearing every day for two months as I lied and told everyone I was okay.

"Are you a doctor?" He crossed his arms over his chest and studied me with intense curiosity.

"No, I'm not a doctor," I snapped and crossed my arms to match his. I was exhausted and not in the mood to deal with whatever this was.

Perhaps he had good intentions and was simply asking a question, but part of me knew that there was more to it than that. There was judgment lingering in the air between us that I had been dealing with from men in my life for as long as I could remember. The constant feeling of needing to explain myself before they took my word to be good enough.

"Exactly— you need to get to the hospital and—"

"I'm a trauma nurse and I see stuff like this every day in the ER. I've been doing this for 5 years and know the signs and symptoms of what to watch for. There is no need for us to risk our lives by going out in this storm for them to tell you the same thing I'm telling you now." My tone was firm as I stood my ground, trembling on the inside as a quick burst of adrenaline shot through me. It was the truth though, I had been watching Annie from the moment we got into his truck, looking for any signs that I should be concerned with.

"Fine, it's your call. I'll be back with your stuff in a few minutes." He turned and walked out the door to the garage, leaving me in silence and alone with my thoughts. When he came back with the duffle bags, he set them down and mumbled goodnight as he stalked off down the hall and upstairs where I heard a door close behind him. I pushed the bags to the side with my foot so they were out of the way before I leaned down to adjust Annie on the couch.

I looked down, her beautiful face was angelic with her brown hair fanned out on the pillow, her skin a soft ivory color. I reached out and gently touched the bruise that was fading on her cheek before I wiped away the tear that slid down my face. I pulled in a deep breath and forced myself to release it slowly, the way I had learned to do it during my therapy sessions. This wasn't the time or the place for a breakdown so I tucked the blanket into the back of the couch and placed a soft kiss on her forehead before climbing into the recliner and closing my eyes. It was strange but for the first time in months, I felt oddly safe and for once, I slept peacefully.

Three
Grant

The house was eerily quiet when I woke up, sending me into a panic when I didn't hear Liam's cartoons blaring from the living room, the tell-tell sign it was Sunday. As suddenly as the fear washed over me, it evaporated just the same when I remembered that he had stayed the night with my mom after I had to run out of town to help a friend fix their furnace before the storm hit.

I rolled out of bed and stretched, my back and neck super achy and sore as I remembered the impact I felt when my truck hit the tree. I ran a hand over my shoulder as I slowly rolled my neck a few times until I heard the pop that provided the relief I was looking for. I pulled the curtain back and looked outside, confirming that at least 12 inches of new snow had fallen since we got home last night.

We. The word hit me like a ton of bricks, forcing back all of the thoughts and feelings I struggled with last night as I tried to fall asleep. I pulled a hoodie over my head and worked my jaw back and forth as I pictured the beautiful woman and her daughter that were still downstairs. In my house. I let out a heavy sigh before grabbing my cell phone and shoving it into the pocket of my sweatpants.

Quietly, I went downstairs, hoping I wouldn't wake them as the stairs softly creaked beneath my weight. I paused outside the living room and glanced in to see both were still sound asleep. Annie's arms were stretched out above her head as she slept sprawled out on the couch, while Lacey was curled up into a ball in the recliner with a throw blanket barely covering her.

I shook my head as I walked into the kitchen, disappointed in myself for not being a better host, and making sure they had things they might need— like blankets. That was where Renee really shined, she was the perfect host and always thought of the little details that would make someone feel welcomed and comfortable. She was the better half of me and some days I was furious that she was taken from me and I was left with the qualities that I hated the most about myself.

Luckily, Annie still had the blanket covering her that I had given her in the truck. The blanket Lacey was using was one of Liam's old blankets that he had outgrown years ago but refused to part with. He insisted on keeping it in the living room for when he wanted to stay up late watching movies, which was every single weekend since Thanksgiving break. School would be starting up again soon once winter break was over and would put a damper on how often we were able to do that.

I walked lightly through the kitchen and started a pot of coffee, not knowing if Lacey was a coffee drinker. Trying to be a better host, I decided to make a full pot and hope that she was so that I wouldn't feel inclined to drink the entire pot by myself. I stood by the sink and watched as the snow fell peacefully while the aroma filled the room and floated down the hallway.

My head whipped around as I heard footsteps behind me as Lacey walked in and joined me. There were dark circles under her eyes which made me wonder if she had slept any last night. Her brown hair was piled loosely on her head, slightly messy from sleeping in the chair. Or at least trying to. She covered her mouth as she yawned and tried to look away. When she finished, she turned back toward me and smiled shyly as if she felt as uncomfortable about being there as I felt having her there.

"Coffee?" I offered as I held up an empty mug out for her. Her long fingers reached out and grabbed it, a warm smile on her face as she pulled it to her chest and waited for me to finish pouring my cup. I walked around to the other side of the island and opened the fridge to grab the creamer as she poured.

I slid the bottle along the countertop to her but she subtly shook her head no as she lifted her mug and took a sip. My eyebrows rose in surprise given that she didn't strike me as the kind of woman who drank her coffee piping hot and black.

"You like your coffee black," I said attempting to make small talk as I nodded in approval and took a sip, suddenly feeling like less of a man for adding creamer to mine.

"Just like my soul," she teased and lowered the mug. I stopped to look at her in the light, finally able to see what she looked like now that she wasn't hidden in the darkness. Her eyes were a beautiful hazel-green color which left me staring harder than I intended as I tried to figure out if they were more green or brown. I looked away to keep from making her uncomfortable and walked to the open space between the kitchen and living room to check on Annie.

It was more out of habit from doing it with Liam than anything but as I looked at Annie, my stomach dropped when I saw a rather decent sized bruise on her cheek. I wondered how I missed it last night but remembered that I didn't get to see her in the light much either. The parental instincts in me kicked in and before I knew it my temper was flaring as I turned around and locked eyes with Lacey.

"How did she get the bruise on her cheek?" I nodded toward Annie, trying to keep any anger or judgment out of my voice.

"It must have been from the accident. She always has a handful of toys in the backseat with her, something must have hit her during the impact." She looked away nervously and something pulled deep in my gut that told me she was full of shit.

"Really?" I tilted my head and studied her, waiting for her to give in and tell me the truth. "You think she has a bruise on her cheek from an accident that barely happened less than eight hours ago?" Something was off, I could feel it. I didn't want to scare her off by accusing her of anything, but I also couldn't just turn the other way if this little girl was in danger and being abused.

She watched me cautiously as I continued to watch her with the same intensity.

"Look, I don't know you. I don't know where you came from. I don't know what your story is. But I do know that that little girl isn't going anywhere until I know what happened to her. A child her age shouldn't have a bruise that big on her face. I can't in good conscience turn my head and look the other way if she's in trouble which means I have no choice but to get Child Protective Services involved." My tone was firm and steady as I walked over and stood in the doorway, blocking her from leaving the kitchen as she set her coffee cup down and started toward the living room. I needed her to talk to me, to reassure me that I wasn't crazy for thinking that she might have caused the bruise on Annie's face.

"You can't be serious," she scoffed. "I told you, it was from the car accident. I already have bruises from it, see?" She tilted her head back to show me her neck. Black marks were starting to cover her skin from the impact of her flying into the steering wheel and having the airbag hit beneath her face.

"Most of your bruises can be explained by the car accident, not all of them." I gave her a knowing look and watched as she looked down and avoided eye contact. My stomach started to twist in knots as I read the truth in what she wasn't saying.

"There's a handful of bruises along your throat that are not from the accident. And they look like they're a few days old. So, what's going on?" I took a step back and leaned against the doorway. I didn't want to have to call the cops on her but there was absolutely no way that I was going to turn my head and look the other way when I had a little girl sleeping on my couch with a decent sized bruise on her face that I was now pretty sure it had something to do with her mom. If she wasn't responsible for it, why not just tell me what happened? She seemed to be working rather hard to keep it a secret and that made me very suspicious.

She glanced behind me to check on her daughter before looking at me. There was a look of worry on her face that I wanted to associate with being a concerned parent, but everything was still too foggy to see clearly.

"Lacey, what happened to Annie?" My tone was softer as I hoped she would give in and talk to me, allow me to help her with whatever was happening.

"I can't get into it, okay? But she's safe with me. I promise you that." She started to tap her foot impatiently as I saw her look past me again.

"That's not good enough for me to just look the other way and let you leave once this storm passes. I need to know that she's not in danger."

A look of panic flashed across her face, her eyes darting up to meet mine, as I said the word I didn't want to say. Danger. Something was wrong.

My anger and frustration were starting to build as I pushed off from the wall and took two strides toward her, catching her off guard as I stood face to face with her.

"I'm not going to keep asking, damn it! I'm a man of little patience and if there is something or someone that you're running from — I need to know about it. Now!" I growled as I caught a glimpse of fear in her eyes before she pulled her shoulders back and pushed her chest out to make herself look taller next to me. I immediately felt the impact of my reaction and knew that I had just forced her even further away. I let out a heavy sigh and waited for the tongue lashing she was about to give me.

"You don't know me. You have no idea who I am or what I'm going through. So why don't you deflate your ego and stop acting like some big, badass guy who's going to make me do something I don't want to?" She stared at me as she spoke, each word crisp with anger. "I appreciate you sheltering us from the storm, but your help ends there. It would be better for everyone if we kept our distance and respected each other's boundaries." She glared at me as she pushed past me and walked away, sitting down on the floor in front of where Annie was still sleeping on the couch.

I blew out the frustrated breath I had been holding as I turned and walked upstairs, needing some space from this infuriating woman. Whether she wanted my help or not, she was going to get it.

16

Four
Lacey

I leaned back against the couch, making sure I didn't wake Annie, and closed my eyes as my head rested on the cushion. For once I wanted to just stop everything and take a moment to breathe. To think. To process everything that had happened in the last two months when my world was first turned upside down while everything was still crashing around me.

I tried to focus on my breathing, pulling in slow, cleansing breaths, and forcing out the frustration and irritation that Grant had just created. Maybe his name should be Gonad, given how he had acted when he didn't get his way. I don't know if he was just a naturally entitled person or if something had happened in his life that made him think that the world owed him something, but I wasn't in the mood to deal with his bullshit. I had plenty of problems of my own, including figuring out how to get another car so we could get the hell out of town as soon as possible.

My anxiety started to rise as I thought about the accident and the storm last night, suddenly feeling more grateful that he had been there when he was. I realized as I started to calm down that my anger wasn't actually with him- he hadn't done anything wrong other than push a little too hard to find out what had happened to Annie. I couldn't blame him though, as a mother I would have been just as concerned if I had met a random woman with a child that had the kind of bruise on her face that Annie had. My anger was with myself for allowing everything to happen that had happened, and worst of all – for letting Annie get caught up in the middle of it.

My breathing started to level out as I tried to remember what had happened, how I lost control of the car so quickly. I wasn't a reckless driver, and having grown up in Colorado, I was used to this type of weather. I relaxed as I let my mind wander, not focusing on anything in particular as I felt my body give in, needing to rest. I sunk further and let Annie's light snores lull me to sleep.

"Get your hands off of her, now!" I screamed as I watched in horror, my hands desperately reaching out to try to grab her and pull her back. His eyes were black, the anger and hatred in them masked by the smell of stale beer on his breath.

"You don't tell me what to do!" His voice boomed through the room, rattling the picture frames on the wall behind him.
I lunged forward and grabbed Annie, pulling her away from him. I immediately noticed the red marks around her arm from how hard he had been holding her. In an instant, rage surged through me as I looked from her back to him. As quickly as I could, I pushed her behind me before I pulled my arm back and swung, hearing the shattering sound as I felt my fist make contact with his cheek. His head whipped back before he shook it off and turned to face me.

I stood in front of Annie, blocking her the best that I could while waiting for him to strike. Flashbacks of my childhood came flooding through and I was thankful for the reminder of what he was capable of. My chest heaved, trying to plan out our next move while knowing that I only had a few seconds. I slightly turned my head to the side so Annie could hear me without taking my eyes off of him.

"Run, Annie, go! Now! Don't look back, run to the car, and get inside!" I yelled loud enough for her to hear me. I felt her fingers tremble as she let go of the back of my shirt and took off running. There wasn't much room with stuff scattered everywhere, but she ran as I told her to. I watched as his eyes shifted to her, the anger prominent again before he kicked the coffee table out of the way to try to get to her.

I jumped in front of him, shielding her body from his reach when I heard a commotion behind me. As we crashed to the floor, I looked over and saw that Annie had fallen, catching her cheek on the end of the coffee table that had been kicked into her path at the last second. She looked at me, eyes wide with fear.

"Run!" My voice screeched through the room as I saw her lip tremble before she got up, grabbed her stuffed puppy, and ran out of the house. The door slammed behind her, reassuring me that she was safe.

"You stupid bitch!" He grunted as his hands wrapped tightly around my throat. I dug my nails in and clawed as hard as I could, trying to get him off of me. "If you're going to live under my roof, you're going to do as I say!"

I tried to turn my head, desperate for a breath as he pushed down harder on my throat. The smell of the beer on his breath was another reminder of my childhood which forced a memory of my mother laying on the floor in this same position. I swore that I would never have the same tragic fate when I watched the life drain from her face as she cried when she saw me watching.

It took everything I had in me to just let go and allow him to think that he had won. He was over three hundred pounds and stronger than me. There was no way of fighting him or getting out from under the weight of his drunk body. I said a quick prayer for Annie as I closed my eyes and let my body relax. I held my breath for what felt like an eternity as I waited for him to notice I wasn't fighting anymore. He chuckled as he rolled off of me, leaving me for dead.

"Annie, you get your ass back here right now!" he yelled, walking toward the front door. Pushing through the lack of oxygen that hadn't yet been replaced, I forced myself to get up. I could hear him down the hallway, opening and closing the doors as he looked for her. As he rounded the corner he saw me standing by the front door with a baseball bat in my hand.

His face started to change as a cruel smile pulled across his face, his laugh starting to rise out of his chest. I swung the bat as hard as I could, knocking him to the ground. I didn't wait to see if he had gotten up before I sprinted out the front door and ran to the shed behind the house. I swung the door open and frantically looked around, straining to listen for the sound of the front door. My eyes wildly searched the shelf in front of me before finding what I needed.

I ran back to the house as quickly as I could, glancing at the car to see Annie's head in the backseat. I picked up the pace and ran the last few steps before swinging the front door open and expecting to see him standing on the other side. A small gasp escaped my throat as I looked down and saw him lying face down in a puddle of blood. My hand trembled as I unscrewed the top of the gas can and started to shake it back and forth, allowing it to soak into the carpet. I let out a shaky breath as I glanced at his body lying lifeless on the floor before striking a match and letting it fall. Within seconds I watched the flames spread, the heat engulfing me.

I sprung forward, gasping for air as I woke up from the nightmare. My eyes frantically scanned the room, confused as I tried to figure out where I was. Voices quietly floated in from the kitchen and I blew out a ragged breath as I started to remember. I held my hand to my chest, trying to calm myself as I turned to check on Annie when I felt her moving behind me. Her eyes softly fluttered open, looking around before spotting me as she smiled.

"Good morning, mommy," her little voice whispered.

"Good morning, princess. How did you sleep?" I turned around and faced her, taking a moment to look her over again.

"Good but I'm kind of sore. My neck hurts." She winced as she reached up to touch it and I saw a burn on her shoulder by her neck from where the seatbelt had been.

"I'm sorry baby, I'll see if I have some Tylenol. How do you feel otherwise?"

"I'm good, you don't have to worry about me, mommy." She smiled and pulled her puppy into her chest as she squeezed it.

"Okay, good. Well, let me find you some Tylenol, and then I'll see about getting us a ride to go get some breakfast." I softly patted her shoulder as I stood up at the same time Grant walked in with a little boy behind him that looked just like him. I quickly realized that I knew nothing about him and wondered if there was a wife he was hiding along with the child that had magically appeared.

"Good morning, ladies, this is my son, Liam." He stepped to the side and pulled him under his arm as the boy tried to wrestle his way out from his dad's embrace.

"Daaadddd," he groaned as a blush crept up his neck. "You're embarrassing me."

"Sorry, my bad," he joked and held his hands up in the air, letting go. I smiled at the interaction, surprised to see this playful side of him.

"I'm Lacey, and this is my daughter, Annie," I said, nodding to the couch as she sat up and waved. Liam smiled and waved back which got a giggle out of Annie.

"My dad made pancakes for breakfast, do you want to come eat then we can watch cartoons?" Liam asked Annie.

I felt my heart skip a beat as the anxiety started to work its way through me again.

"Sure!" Annie exclaimed excitedly as she jumped off the couch. I quickly reached out and gently grabbed her, pulling her back to me.

"Thank you for the offer, that's very sweet. I'm actually going to find a ride and then we'll be out of your hair before you know it." I smiled as I wrapped my arms around Annie, feeling the warmth of her back from being wrapped in the blanket, against my stomach.

"I hate to break it to you— you're not getting a ride. No one is going out in this weather today unless they have to." Grant leaned against the doorframe and nodded toward the window behind me. I squinted my eyes to see through the sheer curtains, dread filling me when I saw the amount of snow that had fallen. He was right, no one was going out in this.

"I made plenty of breakfast for everyone, let's go eat before it gets cold." He cocked an eyebrow as he looked at me, a silent plea for me not to fight him on this. I let my shoulders fall as I nodded and looked out the window again. There were worse things that could happen than to have breakfast with an incredibly good looking stranger and his son.

We followed them into the kitchen and I guided Annie to a chair at the table as they sat down on the opposite side. After she was situated, I picked up the plate in front of her and eyed the options that had been set out on the table. I must have been in a deep sleep because I completely missed him making bacon, eggs, sausage, pancakes, and hash browns. Everything smelled delicious as my stomach growled in anticipation.

Soon everyone had their plates and were busy eating when I caught Grant looking at Annie and subtly shaking his head before looking down to take a bite. I knew how it had to look, to see a child with a bruise like that on her face. There was no way that I could tell him what had really happened, not until it was safe. And honestly, there was no way to know if we would ever be safe.

"How was your slumber party at Nana's?" Grant asked Liam in between bites, a feeling of relief washing over me that he had redirected his attention.

"It was fun, we stayed up late watching movies and eating junk food." His smile spread across his face, revealing a missing tooth up top.

"How's that any different than what you do here?" Grant laughed as he tore off a small piece of bacon and tossed it into his mouth.

"Nana lets me watch the movies you won't let me watch," Liam said dramatically, forcing a giggle out of me as I watched Grant's shocked expression.

"Oh really?"

"Na, not really. But Nana is a lot more fun. She doesn't snore as loud as you do when you guys fall asleep in the middle of the movie."

"I don't snore." Grant lifted his glass and took a drink as he playfully stared at Liam and challenged him to disagree. Liam smirked as he turned and looked directly at me.

"He snores. Like a bear. I'm surprised you didn't hear him last night."

I laughed and turned my head to keep from choking on my bite.

"I was too tired to notice," I teased, briefly looking away from Liam to Grant. He arched an eyebrow as he smiled, the dimple making another appearance.

"So what was Wyatt doing at Nana's this morning?" Grant asked, turning his attention back to Liam as the flirty smile I saw a second ago started to vanish.

"He wanted to check on her to make sure the heater was working."

"How did he get volunteered to bring you home? I was planning to come get you at eight."

"I asked, he agreed." Liam shrugged his shoulders as he shoved a bite of pancake into his mouth. "Besides, his girlfriend lives down the street so it was practically on his way anyways."

Grant laughed as he shook his head and took a sip of coffee. It was interesting to see the dynamic between him bind his son but it left me curious as to what their story was. Neither of them had mentioned his mom so I kept my mouth shut and gave them the same respect for their privacy that I prayed Grant would give me.

After everyone was done eating, the kids asked permission to go watch cartoons in the living room. As they cleared out of the room, I worked on piling the dirty dishes on the table to take to the sink. Grant walked up beside me and grabbed the other pile I had made before turning and carrying them to sink.

"You don't have to clean up, you can go sit with the kids and relax if you want to," he said over his shoulder as he set the dishes on the counter and turned on the water in the sink.

"I'm not leaving you to do the dishes after you cooked breakfast for everyone," I scoffed as I carried the other pile over and set them next to his.

"Why not?" He pulled his brows together in confusion.

"Because that's rude!" I turned and leaned back against the counter so I could see his face. "If you would scoot out of the way, I can wash those for you." I pushed my lips together into an awkward duck-kissy face pose and hoped it would make me look cute enough to get my way.

"I'm not washing all of these," he said matter-of-factly as he rinsed each plate and set it on the other side. "I'm just rinsing them, that's what the dishwasher is for." He nodded to the side so I leaned forward and looked at it.

"Okay," I said, pushing off from the counter. "You rinse, I'll load." I walked over and opened the dishwasher, pulling the bottom rack out when his hand reached out and stopped me.

"Thank you, but it's fine. I'll load it."

I let out a loud, frustrated sigh as I crossed my arms over my chest and glared at him.

"What's your problem?" I demanded.

"I don't have a problem. I like to do things a certain way and you're a guest in my house. Guests don't do chores." He shrugged as he turned his head back to focus on rinsing the rest of the dishes.

"Do you not think that I'm capable of loading a dishwasher?"

"I don't know what you're capable of or not. What I do know is that I will do the cleaning. If you want to hang out and talk, that's fine. You can start by explaining what happened last night." He reached over to turn off the water before drying his hands and tossing the towel on the counter as he turned around to look at me.

We stood staring at each other for what felt like minutes before I heard Liam call for him to come fix the internet that had gone out again. His shoulders fell slightly as he pursed his lips as he debated whether to say whatever he was going to say before he left. I let out a shaky breath as I felt the air in the room change once he was gone. I said a silent prayer that this storm would pass as quickly as it came so I could get the hell out of here before things got too complicated. I quickly loaded the dishwasher with the dishes from the sink, feeling somewhat satisfied that he didn't get his way. As childish as it seemed, this guy pushed every button I had and I found it getting progressively harder not to push his.

<u>Five</u>
Grant

The day went by at a slow pace, perfect for a lazy Sunday. After I got the internet restarted for Liam, I went back into the kitchen to find that Lacey had finished loading the dishwasher and started it as she acted nonchalant, drinking coffee while watching the snow fall outside. While it had irritated me that she didn't listen when I had asked her not to do the dishes, I found that I wasn't as angry as I thought I would be.

Control was a major issue for me and had been ever since Renee died and sent my life spinning out of control. How are you supposed to feel in control of anything when your world shatters around you and you have to pick up the pieces before they fall because a child is depending on you? After losing Renee I made sure that I was constantly in control of everything, even the tiniest details. Not just for me, but for Liam. It was a very delicate balance that needed constant attention to keep everything from falling apart.

I glanced across the room at Lacey who was curled up in the recliner with her legs tucked under her while she watched the kids play a video game that Annie had chosen. I hadn't seen Liam play this game in months, but he lit up the moment Annie asked if they could play it and insisted that he knew all of the tricks to help them beat the bad guy. Lacey's face was pointed at the tv which made it look like she was watching it but the worry in her eyes gave her away. She was somewhere else completely, worrying about something that she refused to talk to me about.

I had gone back and forth over things in my head all morning as I cooked breakfast, sneaking a quick look into the living room as they slept, trying to figure out what she could be hiding. Who she could be running from. The problem-solver in me wanted to do just that-solve the problem. Whatever it was, I could help her fix it. But when I put myself in her shoes, I remembered how reluctant I was to accept anyone's help after Renee died so I didn't blame her for not wanting to talk to a stranger about her problems.

The thing that kept eating away at me was the bruise on Annie's face. I had seen plenty of bruises in my lifetime, growing up as a middle child with two brothers, as well as being a P.E. teacher for elementary school kids. The bruise that Annie had on her cheek was long and didn't match what I expected to see if someone had hit her. It almost looked like she had run into something, or possibly had something hit her. I considered Lacey's explanation that a toy had flown up and hit her during the accident but it looked like it had been there a little bit longer than that.

My attention was redirected when I heard clapping and a giggle from Annie as Liam slammed his controller down on the couch next to him before getting up to do a victory dance. The image on the screen showed a bad guy laying on the ground with stars circling his head, confirming that they had defeated the big boss that they had been talking about for the past hour. I glanced at the time on my phone, debating whether I should be the tough dad and stick with cutting Liam off for the day since he had already been playing for a few hours, or if I should make an exception and let him play a little bit longer given we had company and I didn't have anything else to entertain them with. Besides, it was New Year's Eve, why not let them go out with a bang on the last day of the year.

I felt my phone vibrate and looked down to see Chase's name on the screen. I slid my finger across the screen to unlock it as I lifted myself off the floor and walked into the kitchen to answer it.

"Hey, what's up?" I said as I refilled my cup of coffee and took a sip.

"Just wanted to check in to see what you and Liam were up to tonight and if you guys wanted to hang out and ring in the new year together?"

I glanced back into the living room as I thought about it. While it would be good to see them and celebrate New Years together like we always did, it felt weird to tell him that we had unexpected guests staying with us. I could make something up to avoid having to tell anyone, but I knew that Liam had been looking forward to seeing them tonight. There wasn't much that he looked forward to these days so I couldn't bring myself to take this away from him. As I was about to speak, I saw Lacey coming toward me, her eyes locked on mine as she froze in her tracks when she noticed I was on the phone. I nodded and waved for her to come in as I turned around in my seat so I could focus on the conversation instead of what she was doing.

"Yeah, we can still hang out and celebrate the new year. Did you guys want to come here or is it too hard to take Rylee out in this storm?" I tried to keep my voice low so Lacey wouldn't hear but it was nearly impossible as the room was completely silent aside from the sound the water made as it filled her glass.

"We can go there if that works for you guys, the storm isn't too bad and we only live ten minutes away."

"Sounds good. Have you talked to Noah and Jade to see if they're coming too?" I asked, glancing at Lacey out of the corner of my eye as she filled a second glass with water.

"Not yet, I'll call him when we hang up and let him know the plan."

"Okay," I sighed, taking in a deep breath. "Oh, and Chase?"

"Yeah?"

"We have company tonight, just so you guys know." I gritted my teeth as I said it, noticing the moment Lacey's body tightened in response as she heard it.

"You do? Who?" There was genuine curiosity in his voice as he asked it which meant that he was going to give me shit about this and read more into it than what it was.

"A woman named Lacey and her daughter, Annie. They were in a car accident last night and are stranded due to the weather, so they're staying with us since all of the hotels are booked." I ran a hand through my hair and leaned back against the chair.

"Grant Fucking Walker has a woman in his house? No fucking way!"

I rolled my eyes and looked out the window as I listened to Chase laughing his ass off on the other line.

"Just be here by 8," I snapped and hung up the phone. I set it on the table in front of me as I slowly turned to look at Lacey. She still had her back to me as she wiped down the counter. I watched as she lifted the towel to put it back on the hook above the sink, her fingers trembling as she did. When she turned around holding both glasses of water, there was a look of worry on her face.

"I'm sorry, I wasn't trying to eavesdrop on your phone call but I couldn't help but overhear your plans for tonight. Annie and I will find somewhere to go and will be out of your hair in no time." She smiled like she was embarrassed as she started to walk out of the room.

"Lacey," I said before she could leave, feeling relieved when she stopped and turned around. Her eyes looked up and met mine. "I really hope that you and Annie will feel comfortable hanging out with my family tonight, we would love to celebrate the new year with you."

A smile quickly washed across her face before she looked away. When she looked back, her face was back to the solemn expression she had been wearing all day.

"Thank you, but we don't want to be in the way." She offered a tight smile as she waited to make sure I was done before she turned to leave.

"You won't be in the way, it's just a laid back group of people, hanging out and celebrating the new year. They'll be here around 8."

"Okay. Thank you." She licked her lips nervously before turning and walking into the living room. I watched as she handed a glass of water to Annie and took a drink out of her own. I could hear the excitement in Annie's voice when she asked her mom if they were really staying with us for a New Year's Eve party. Lacey subtly looked up at me before answering her, nodding as Annie set her glass on the coffee table before reaching up to wrap her arms around her mom's neck as she hugged her. I felt a pull deep in my chest that I hadn't felt in a long time as I watched the kids smile and laugh with Lacey in the other room.

<u>Six</u>
Lacey

It was after seven when we finished dinner and I convinced Grant to let me help with cleaning up. The day had been surprisingly relaxing, which was great given that my body felt like it had been run over by a truck and needed the rest. I had it in my mind that we wouldn't stay long and that I could get us back on the road sooner than later, but when Grant confirmed that the roads in and out of Haven Brook were closed due to the storm, I knew we were stuck for a little while longer.

I was thankful that I had thought enough in advance to pack the duffle bags for Annie and me with the things we would need if we ever had to leave at the last minute. There was a full week's worth of clothes for each of us, as well as a few sentimental items that I made sure to pack. For days, I stared at the duffle bags, praying that I had packed them for nothing; praying that my instincts weren't right and that my mind wasn't playing terrible tricks on me.

I stepped out of the shower and wrapped the towel tightly around my body, shivering from the cold tile under my bare feet. Grant had insisted that Annie and I move our stuff up to Liam's room and use the guest bathroom since we would be staying a few days, at minimum. While Liam seemed happy to give up his room to us, he groaned when he joked about how he wasn't going to get any sleep with how loud his dad snores.

Annie had already taken a quick shower and was sitting anxiously on the floor while I finished mine. I knew she was excited to go downstairs and help get things set up for the party, which I still felt terrible about crashing. My nerves had been fried all day, wondering if Annie was old enough to remember what today was. It was killing me inside and I hoped that she was too little to know that today would have been mine and her father's tenth wedding anniversary. We did a big celebration every year, partly to celebrate the new year, but mostly to celebrate each other.

I got ready quickly while Annie played in the room, pulling my hair up in the front so it was out of my face. My fingers trembled as they worked the bobby pins into place, forcing a cute little bump up in the front as I straightened the pieces that hung to the side of it, framing my face. I didn't have anyone to get dolled up for but I also didn't have the heart to go through with breaking that tradition this year. Things were hard enough already, I wasn't ready to deal with picking up the pieces of my heart when it shattered at the thought that I wouldn't have anyone to celebrate with tonight. No one to make a toast with about how great the new year would be and no one to kiss at the stroke of midnight.

I rubbed my lips together, watching as the red lipstick coated each lip perfectly. I stepped back and ran a hand down the front of my cream-colored sweater dress, wondering what Derek would have thought when he saw me in it. The warmth of a tear trickled down my cheek as I bit my lip to keep from crying. I sucked in a deep breath and forced it out, determined to pull myself together as I spun my wedding ring around nervously on my finger. I heard Liam call for Annie, asking her to come look at the decorations he had found. She quickly peeked in the bathroom, begging me to let her go. I sighed and nodded yes, knowing that I would be down there in a few minutes myself. I didn't like having her away from me, but I was able to hear everything downstairs clearly which made me feel more at ease.
It was 7:30 by the time I finished getting ready and made my way downstairs. I turned the corner to go into the kitchen at the same time Grant was coming out and crashed into him. I braced myself against this broad chest, feeling the solid muscles beneath my fingertips. I felt his hands on my hips as he tried to steady both of us, the warmth of them sending a chill through my body. My eyes fluttered open as I slowly looked up, taking in his blue eyes as he looked down at me.

"You okay?" he asked quietly, his voice scratching in the back of his throat while his hands still held onto me.

"Yeah, I'm good." I parted my lips to speak but the words caught in my throat as I watched his eyes wander down my body, a look of lust on his face. My body felt like it was on fire under his gaze, paralyzing me in place as he took his time soaking in every tiny detail.

"Hey, Dad, can we hang up some streamers for decoration?" Liam called from the kitchen, breaking his focus. His head snapped up as he listened before agreeing to let Liam do what he wanted. Slowly he pulled his hands away from my body and clenched his fists at his sides as he appeared to struggle with not reaching out and touching me again. I tucked a strand of hair behind my ear, more out of nervous habit than anything.

"You look nice," he said as stepped to the side to let Liam pass by as he ran upstairs to get the supplies he needed.

"Thank you." I smiled as I ran a hand over my stomach, suddenly feeling nervous and self-conscious that I was probably the only one who was going to be dressed up. Maybe this was a big mistake after all. My palms started sweating as I fought the urge to run upstairs, crawl in a corner, and cry. I could feel the anxiety building as my bottom lip started to tremble, knowing that I was about to lose any control that I had left.

"Hey, what's wrong?" His eyes were sympathetic as he studied me.

"Nothing, I'm just a little anxious about crashing your party and meeting your friends. And I'm pretty sure that I'm way overdressed. I should go change," I rambled as I quickly turned to go back upstairs. His hand reached out and gently grabbed my elbow, holding me in place as he took a step forward.

"I'm sorry that you're feeling anxious, but I promise they are really cool people and you'll feel like part of the gang in no time. Plus, they're family, not friends. That means that we don't pretend to be anything or worry about anyone judging us. You're safe here."

I knew that his words were meant to put me at ease with being around new people but the moment that he said I was safe, I knew that I was far from it. The hours had passed by slowly and with each minute I knew the chances of him getting closer and finding us were increasing.

"Thanks, I'm just going to change real quick." I forced a smile and was about to walk away when I saw Annie come around the corner. Her eyes lit up when she saw me, running over to wrap her arms around my waist. Grant smiled warmly as he stepped back to let her in.

"Mama, you look so pretty! I knew it would be like all of the other New Year's where you get dressed up and we have a party!" Her eyes were wide with excitement and I watched in sadness the moment that everything clicked into place for her. Her eyes filled with tears as she looked up at me. "It's not like the other parties, is it mama?"

I shook my head as I held my breath and fought back the tears.

"No, baby, it's not," I whispered.

Annie held onto my waist and hugged me tightly as she turned her head to look at Grant.

"Mommy and daddy always had a big party and played kissy-face all night while we celebrated the new year. But daddy can't be here for this party."

Her face fell and she tucked her head into my stomach as I rubbed her back. Grant looked up at me as a tear slid down my cheek. I bit the inside of my cheek to keep from crumbling to the floor and falling apart.

"I've got the streamers, Annie do you want to help me put them up?" Liam asked as he bounced down the stairs, completely unaware of what had happened. She looked up at me for approval.

"Go ahead, baby. Go have fun and make everything look really pretty," I said as my voice cracked. She smiled and let go as she walked with Liam to go hang the decorations in the living room. When they were out of sight I let out the breath that I had been holding. I forced a tight smile at Grant before I turned and walked away. I could hear him say my name as I went upstairs, not having the strength to talk about what happened.

<u>Seven</u>
Grant

The night was turning out to be an easygoing, relaxing get-together as I had hoped for. Lacey had been quiet the majority of the night so I tried to give her space and not force her to talk about what happened. I was pleasantly surprised that she hadn't changed her dress after all. I didn't know the full story behind what had happened between her and Annie earlier but I could tell that it meant a lot to Lacey for her to get dressed up tonight and continue with a tradition that she had with her husband. Part of me wondered if things had gone sour between them and that's who Lacey was running from, while the other part of me recognized the unmistakable grief that someone has when they've lost someone close to them: a spouse.

Everyone was gathered around in the living room, spread out between the couch and the floor while the kids played with Rylee who had just started to walk. I glanced over at my brother and saw the adoring look he was giving his wife, Mia, and felt a bit jealous of the life they had together. I was happy for them, that wasn't the problem. It was that they represented everything that I would never have – a constant companion to share their life with and grow old together as they made new memories with the family they created.

"So, what's the plan for Ry's birthday?" Noah asked, interrupting my thoughts. He was sitting in the recliner with Jade on his lap as she twirled a stray piece of hair around her finger. It was a nervous habit she tried to break but hadn't. I watched as her blonde hair wrapped tightly around her finger before she would unwind it and start over again. I looked away before I got lost in the hypnotizing trance. "We're just doing something small, cake and ice cream with the family, next Saturday at our house," Chase said as he pulled Mia closer to him on the couch.

"What? It's her first birthday— you're not going all out for it?" Noah teased, trying to get a rise out of Chase. They were best friends who gave each other shit like brothers.

"I'm too tired for a big party," Mia sighed before her eyes went wide with panic. She chewed her bottom lip as she looked up at Chase who was chuckling and shaking his head.

"You might as well tell them," he said quietly in her ear, loud enough that we could hear. I laughed as Liam's head quickly turned in their direction, excited to hear that someone had a secret.

"Tell us what?" His voice was higher than normal with excitement.

Mia studied Chase's face as he slowly nodded yes and planted a kiss on her forehead.

"Okay, um," she hesitated. "Rylee is going to be a big sister!" She smiled as Chase rubbed a hand over her belly, a small bump showing against the thin fabric of the dress she was wearing. I shifted my attention to Liam, watching as the emotions flashed across his face before he got up and went over to hug them. I felt eyes on me as I looked over and watched Lacey as she took everything in. The look on my face must have spoken some secret words that only she could understand as she gave me an empathetic smile before looking over at Liam. I hadn't told her about Renee but she wasn't stupid and had to have noticed that there wasn't a woman in his life given that we hadn't talked about one.

The room got noisy as everyone said congratulations and got settled again. I looked over at Jade and Noah, wondering how she was taking the news of Mia being pregnant. I knew that finding out that Chase and Mia were having another baby was hard for Liam and I, knowing that we would never know what it felt like to have another child on the way. I could only imagine what Jade was feeling, hearing that her best friend was pregnant again, less than a year after Jade had lost a baby.

Noah leaned forward and whispered something in Jade's ear as he gently rubbed his hands up and down her arms. I couldn't hear what he was saying but I watched as Jade listened, a smile pulling tightly across her face as she nodded. She shrugged her shoulders and leaned her head back against his chest. He smiled broadly as he looked around the room, waiting for the right time to get everyone's attention.

"Jade and I have a little announcement we would like to make as well," he said as his voice boomed through the room. Everyone got quiet and turned to look at them. "We've decided to move the wedding up to March, instead of September."

"Didn't want to do it in the heat after all?" Chase asked, chuckling as if he knew he was right. Noah and Jade had been engaged for 9 months and couldn't agree on when to get married. Noah and Jade looked at each other, a smirk on his face as she rolled her eyes. As she looked back at everyone in the room, she smiled and took a deep breath.

"We've moved it to March because we're having a baby in June," she said slowly as she forced it out in one long-winded breath as she placed a hand on her stomach.

Mia's hand clasped over her mouth as her eyes filled with tears. The room was quiet as everyone took in the news, my attention shifting back to Liam again. He tried to keep the hurt off his face as he forced a smile and came over to hug Noah and Jade. Everyone was up and moving, giving hugs and pats on the back, while I stayed sitting on the floor. Everyone's lives were changing and moving forward while we were frozen in place.

The night went by at a fast pace after that. While the women sat and talked about due dates and cravings, the guys retreated to the kitchen to drink beer and bullshit. I was relieved that Lacey had jumped into the conversation with the girls, knowing that Mia and Jade were two of the nicest women I had ever known. The clock wound down and soon it was time to ring in the new year. We all gathered around in the living room as I turned the TV on and found a channel to watch the ball drop.

"Mama, can I kiss Liam at midnight or is that not okay?" Annie asked Lacey, catching her off guard. Lacey looked at me with panic on her face, unsure of what to do. I shrugged my shoulders because the hell if I knew what to do.

"I think a kiss on the cheek would be fine if it's okay with Liam, and his dad," Lacey replied cautiously, allowing me to veto her decision.

"That's fine with me, buddy," I said, smiling at Liam as he looked up at me.

"Yay! And you and Mr. Grant can kiss too!" Annie exclaimed excitedly.

Lacey and I looked at each other nervously before she shifted her attention back to Annie.

"No, honey, we're not going to kiss," she said softly, gently reaching out and brushing a thumb across the girl's cheek.

"Why not? You can have a friend's kiss, like me and Liam. Otherwise, you will be the only two who don't kiss at New Year's and that's bad luck, mama." She looked up at Lacey with sadness in her eyes.

"I would be honored to share a good luck, friends' kiss with you," I said softly, pulling Lacey's attention back to me as Annie squealed. She studied my face, a concern on hers that I couldn't quite read. The countdown on the TV started as everyone yelled out the numbers together.

"Seventeen!"
"Sixteen!"
"Fifteen!"

"We don't have to if it makes you uncomfortable," I offered, trying to read what she was thinking.

"No, it's okay," she sighed and pulled her shoulders back.

"Ten!"
"Nine!"
"Eight!"

"Are you sure?" I stepped closer, my fingers itching to touch her as my mind screamed for me to stop.

"Five!"
"Four!"
"Three!"
"Two!"

I reached out and wrapped an arm behind her waist as I gently lowered my lips to hers. I could feel the warmth as she let out a shaky breath, her lips gently parting as she kissed me back. Her lips were soft and suddenly I felt the need to kiss her deeper, to feel her kiss me back. Her hand wrapped around my neck as her fingers gently ran through my hair. I wanted to pull away but the pull to her was stronger. My lips pressed harder against hers, excitement flooding through me when she pressed hers into mine and parted her lips to allow my tongue access. I softly licked her lips as I eagerly wanted to explore.

"I don't think friends are supposed to kiss like that," Liam said sarcastically as he walked off with Annie. Lacey and I stepped apart as she quickly brought her hand to her mouth, replacing where my lips had just been. I wanted to say something to her, to apologize for crossing the line, but when I went to open my mouth she was already gone and rushing upstairs.

Everyone left soon after I declined their offers to help with the clean-up. I had wanted to talk to Liam privately, to make sure he was okay, but he was already asleep in my bed by the time I got up there. I felt restless with an excess amount of energy running through me. Knowing I wasn't going to get any sleep anytime soon, I walked downstairs to watch tv for a bit. As I made my way down, I noticed a light on in the bathroom at the end of the hall. Lacey and Annie had gone to bed earlier so I figured someone had left the light on by accident. As I reached to open the door I stopped when I heard crying on the other side. I knocked softly, trying not to startle whoever was on the other side.

A few seconds later I heard the lock turn and the door opened. Lacey stood in front of me wearing a T-shirt and a pair of sweatpants, her hair tossed up in a messy ponytail, with streaks of mascara running down her face. Her nose was red and her cheeks were splotchy from crying. I didn't say anything because I didn't know what to say. The kiss had messed with my head ever since it happened and I was still struggling to figure out how I felt about it. I reached a hand out to her and was surprised when she took it. She stepped out slowly, her body shaking as she started crying again. I wrapped her in my arms and held her. A few minutes later she had calmed down enough to walk with me to the couch. We sat in silence for a few minutes as she sniffled and tried to catch her breath.

"Lacey, I'm really sorry about the kiss earlier. I didn't mean to overstep, and I'm so sorry that it happened." I looked over at her, my face etched with shame.

"The kiss was fine," she pulled in a deep breath, "that's not why I'm... crying..." Her shoulders fell as she started crying again.

"Okay. Do you want to talk about it?" I offered, placing a hand on her knee.

She shook her head as pulled a worn-out tissue out of her pocket and wiped at her face before blowing her nose.

"I'm sorry, I don't mean to be such a mess. Tonight was har…hard… harder than I thought." Her voice rose as she struggled to get the words out before she started crying again. I reached over and placed the palm of my hand on her back, gently patting her like I do when Liam gets upset.

"You don't have anything to be sorry about."

She nodded her head and sucked in a ragged deep breath as she turned to look at me.

"Tonight was supposed to be… my ten-year… anniversary," she said in one long-winded breath. "My husband… was killed…three months ago… in a car accident." Her eyes closed as she said it, her shoulders falling as her body shook the harder she cried. She leaned forward and let her head fall forward as she allowed the grief to take over. I closed my eyes and took a deep breath, trying to think of something to say that could help her feel better but I knew that there wasn't anything that I could say. You don't ever feel better after losing the love of your life.

"I'm so sorry, Lacey," I whispered loud enough for her to hear me as I continued to pat her back.

"I thought I would be okay tonight, I thought I could do it." She turned to look at me, her eyes a darker green than I had ever seen. There was so much sadness in her eyes that I couldn't tell if I was seeing her grief or my own reflected in hers.

"It's hard to know what situations are going to be hard, sometimes they just take you by surprise. That's the unfortunate thing about death, it doesn't care whether our hearts can handle it."

Her eyes searched my face as she listened to my words and I could tell that she knew there was a deeper meaning behind them. Instinctively, I moved my hand away and rubbed at the scruff that was getting thicker on my jawline.

"Liam's mom?" she asked quietly. I nodded, unsure of whether I was ready to talk about this. I took a deep breath as my leg started to bounce nervously. She had opened up to me about something personal and painful, I could try to do the same.

"My wife, Renee. She lost her battle with cancer almost four years ago."

"I'm sorry for your loss," she said as she reached over and squeezed my hand.

I nodded as I tried to blink past the tears that were threatening to come out. I hadn't cried since the day that Renee died and I wasn't going to start again now.

39

40

Eight
Lacey

"Seven. Eight. Nine. Ten. Ready or not, here I come." His voice was low as he spoke the words that should have sounded like a game. I could hear it in his tone that this was going to be anything but fun. I quietly slid back further, trying to keep my skin from sticking to the wood floor beneath me as I hid under the bed.

Mom was at work and dad had been drinking all afternoon which only made him more furious when she called to say she had to work late. It was the last straw for him in his drunken stupor, making him even more irritable than when he was sober. I knew today was going to be a bad day when I walked into the kitchen to fix a bowl of cereal and dad had mom pinned to the wall by her throat again.

His footsteps were heavy, the floor shifting beneath his weight as he walked toward the bed. I pinched my eyes shut and held my breath, praying that he was too drunk to find me. I crossed my fingers and tucked my teddy bear under my arm as I waited it out. Just a few more minutes and he would get frustrated and leave.

My lungs burned as I continued to hold my breath, not willing to risk making any sound that might lead him directly to me. Panic started to rush through me as I worried about passing out, or worse, dying, with no air. Everything around me went silent and I couldn't tell if it was from the pressure in my ears, or if I had lucked out and he had left. I slowly let out the breath, forcing myself to be calm so I wouldn't suck in another one and give away my hiding spot. As the air slowly left my body I felt a hand wrap around my ankle, yanking me out from under the bed.

THE TIES THAT BIND

"Found you," he growled as his eyes turned black as night.

I sprung forward on the bed, clutching my chest as I gasped for air. I quickly looked around the room, looking for him before I recognized the collection of action figures on the shelf beside me and remembered where I was. I glanced down and sighed, relieved that I hadn't woken Annie up.

It wasn't unusual for me to have bad dreams, they had haunted me the majority of my life and always resulted in me waking up, gasping for air. My problem was that I had a hard time figuring out if they were real memories from my childhood or if they were terrible, made up situations that my brain decided to conjure up, just to torture me. Almost all of my nightmares involved my father and I had a hard time knowing what was true and what wasn't.

I shook my head to clear the thoughts as I quietly got out of bed and checked my phone. My stomach dropped when I looked down and saw 3 missed calls from my dad. I had been anxiously waiting for them to come, knowing that he would be pissed about what happened. My dad wasn't one to forgive and forget. He was the ultimate revenge seeker, making sure those who wronged him paid for whatever they did. And I wasn't going to be an exception. The past few days I had held onto the hope that he hadn't called because he hadn't survived but fate seemed determined to prove that evil never dies.

It was still early in the morning and technically it wouldn't hurt to try to sleep some more but my body was too used to getting up this early to go in for my shifts at the hospital. Besides, there was no way I could try to rest now after knowing that my father was actively trying to reach me. There was nothing planned for today, and as I looked outside and saw more snow falling, I knew we would be with Grant for at least one more day. If this storm was as bad as the last one, it would mean that the roads into Haven Brook would be closed a little bit longer, giving us some more time to figure out what to do and where to go. Letting Annie sleep, I tucked my phone into my pocket and crept downstairs, making sure not to wake anyone else up.

As I walked into the kitchen I was surprised to see Grant sitting at the table, drinking a cup of coffee and reading a newspaper. I smiled as I walked in, still feeling somewhat awkward around him after falling apart on New Year's Eve. Several days had passed and yet we hadn't spoken of my breakdown or the kiss.

My lips still tingled every time I thought of the way his had felt against them. I ran a finger over them as I poured a cup of coffee, completely lost in thought. My daydreams had quickly started to shift, leading us to doing more than just kissing, which was an incredibly odd feeling for me. There was a tremendous amount of guilt that weighed on me when I remembered that Derek hadn't been gone 3 months yet, and I was already fantasizing about another man. But the way that Grant made me feel, it was completely different than Derek had ever made me feel.

Things with Derek were great but after we had Annie, things started to fizzle out, just like everyone warns you they will when you have kids. We tried to keep the spark between us but between busy work schedules, very little sleep, and a newborn that needed constant attention, things just started to fall by the wayside. I kept telling myself that things would get better, we would find our way back to each other, but we didn't. We were like best friends who decided to have a baby together. Nothing more and nothing less. I had realized that part of why I loved getting dressed up every year for New Year's Eve was because it was the only time that he was focused on me again. He made me feel beautiful and sexy, but most importantly, I felt wanted.

I was still rubbing my fingers across my lips when I heard the sound of the coffee spilling over, out of my cup. I snapped out of my trance and looked down as I quickly set the pot on the warmer, stepping away before the scalding hot liquid dripped off the counter and onto the floor.

"Shit!" I hissed, frustrated that I hadn't been paying attention. Grant looked up and set his newspaper down before rushing over to help. He grabbed the roll of paper towels off of the counter behind me and reached around to start blotting the counter to keep the coffee from dripping off. My breath hitched as I felt the warmth of his body behind me as he worked quickly to clean up the coffee. I was frozen in place, desperate to clean up my mess, but afraid to move and allow my body to have any more contact with his. A few seconds, later he was still reaching around me, adding more paper towels to the pile on the counter as they soaked up the coffee.

"Are you okay? Did you get burned?" His voice was quiet in my ear as his chest slightly brushed against my back. I had to force myself to remember to breathe so I didn't pass out. Unable to speak, I nodded my head slowly, embarrassed that he had to come to my rescue, yet again.

"Why don't you go sit down and I'll clean this up and bring you your coffee? You look a little frazzled this morning." He gently placed his hand on my lower back, guiding me over to the table. I sat down, thankful that I didn't have to worry about my knees giving out. I wasn't usually the kind of girl who was so physically impacted by an attractive man. For whatever reason, he was having a huge effect on me which meant that we needed to leave and soon.

I watched as he cleaned up the mess, his T-shirt pulling tight across his toned body as he reached forward to wipe up the rest of the coffee. A few minutes later, he threw the last paper towel in the trash and walked over, sitting down across from me at the table. He gently slid my coffee over, eyeing me carefully to make sure I didn't spill it again.

I felt my cheeks flush as I looked away, embarrassed, wrapping the cup in my hands. I pretended to be interested in the snow that had started to fall outside so I could avoid having to look at his disheveled bed hair that had me wanting to run my fingers through it.

"So, what has you all worked up this morning?" He arched an eyebrow and lifted his cup to take a sip. I licked my lips before slowly turning to look at him. Even though I knew it would be hard to look at him and keep the emotions off of my face, I knew it would make it even harder if I avoided him. It would make me look like I was avoiding him, which I was.

"Nothing," I lied. "Bad dreams, that's all." I shrugged as if it was nothing and took a sip, trying to keep myself distracted from the look he was giving me. It was a look that was calling me on my bullshit and challenging me to tell the truth. I had barely started processing the fact that my dad was alive and well, likely soon to be hunting me down. How was I supposed to explain that to him? Of course I was worked up between the random slew of thoughts working through my mind.

"Interesting," he replied casually as he picked up the newspaper and went back to reading it. I pulled my neck back and looked at him, confused about what that was supposed to mean. He didn't say anything that should offend me, but it was HOW he said it that had my temper starting to flare.

"What's that supposed to mean?" I leaned forward and narrowed my eyes at him, waiting for him to lower the newspaper so he could see the glare I was giving him.

"Nothing." He shrugged as he turned the page, seemingly uninterested in the conversation.

"Really?" I let out a loud sigh and crossed my arms over my chest as I leaned back against the chair and stared at him. For a moment I envisioned myself having some sort of superhero powers where I could burn a hole through his stupid newspaper with the amount of heat that was radiating from my glare. As if sensing my frustration, he folded the newspaper and set it down before folding his hands in front of him on the table. He met my glare, not backing down, or looking even the slightest bit bothered by it.

"I find it interesting that you're going with the bad dream excuse when I sat here and watched you run your fingers across your lips while you were lost in some sort of erotic fantasy while spilling coffee all over the counter." He quirked an eyebrow and challenged me to counter what he was saying.

I felt the color drain from my face as his eyes stayed focused on me.

"I wasn't lost in an erotic fantasy," I whispered, looking away.

"Are you sure?" He pulled his bottom lip in between his teeth as he watched my reaction. My heart was racing as my palms started to sweat. I wasn't willing to admit there was a fantasy to myself, let alone to him.

"Yeah, I'm sure." I looked up and met his look, watching as the blue darkened around his pupils.

"Okay, if that's how you want to play this," he said as he stood up and slid his chair under the table. I held my breath, waiting for him to turn and walk away. Instead, he took a step closer and leaned down, locking me in place as one hand held onto the back of my chair and the other planted firmly on the table. He leaned in close enough that I could feel the heat of his breath on my neck as he started to speak.

"Call me crazy, but I thought maybe you were thinking about the kiss we shared the other night. The one we keep avoiding talking about." He paused for a second, letting out a heavy breath that tickled my skin. "And yeah, I would call it an erotic fantasy because fuck if I haven't ever been that turned on by a single kiss."

He straightened and stood next to me, pausing to grab his coffee before he walked away. As he was about to walk out of the room, he turned and looked at me over his shoulder.

"Don't worry, it's fucking with my head too. But that doesn't make it any less real."

I heard him make his way upstairs and a few minutes later the shower was turned on as the sound of running water filled the silence in the kitchen. I was completely stunned by what he had said before he left, especially since I wasn't the only one who had been turned on by that kiss. Butterflies fluttered through my stomach as I briefly entertained the thought of something happening between us. But as quickly as the thought entered my mind, the grief and guilt came rushing back with it.

We moved around each other in silence the rest of the morning as I got ready and he made breakfast once the kids were up. It was the last week of winter break before school started again and I felt anxious about not being able to send Annie to school. I never thought I would actually go through with leaving, so the last minute decision didn't give a lot of time for planning. Even though I daydreamed about us leaving, I only ever focused on the getting far enough away part. I had only thought of getting us to a place that was safe.

My mind raced through all of the worst-case scenarios while I chewed on a piece of bacon and the kids talked about building a snowman. I could feel Grant's eyes on me again but I purposely avoided him as long as I could. After breakfast was done, the kids ran off to the fenced-in backyard to build a snowman.

I glanced out the window so many times to check on Annie that I heard Grant sigh as he slammed his fists down on the counter, pulling my attention away from her. My hand flung up to my chest in surprise, as I tried to figure out what he was so mad about.

"What is going on? And I want the truth, Lacey."

The look on his face was more frustration than anger, but either way, I hated that I was the reason it was there.

"Nothing is going on, I don't know what you're talking about." I walked past him and went to the sink, turned on the water, and started rinsing the pile of dishes on the counter.

I heard his footsteps come up behind me as he reached forward, his chest rock hard and solid against my back, and turned off the water. I let my wet hands rest against the edge of the sink, refusing to turn around and look at him.

"Then why do you keep looking outside every 30 seconds, like someone is going to come take Annie?" His voice was low in my ear.

My shoulders slumped and I let my head hang down as I closed my eyes. I wasn't ready to talk about what happened and yet I was running out of options to keep avoiding it.

"Lacey, I'm going to ask again. What's going on?" His voice was calmer this time as he sounded like he was struggling to control it.

"Nothing," I snapped, whipping around to face him. I pulled in a deep breath and looked at him. "But I do need to get a few things from the store today, I'll check to see if there are any vacancies at the hotel now that the storm has passed through."

He clenched his jaw as he stepped back, allowing me some room to move.

"My keys are on the table by the door, take my truck, and go grab what you need." He shook his head as he walked out of the room. I let out a shaky breath before going outside to ask Annie to go to the store with me. After several moans and groans from her about wanting to play, I gave up and decided to trust Grant when he offered to watch her while I went to the store. I reached into my pocket to silence my cell phone without bothering to check the caller ID as I grabbed his keys and went out through the garage. I hopped into the truck and waited for the door to finish opening before I pulled out and made my way to the only store in town.

48

Nine
Grant

Lacey had been gone a few hours when the kids decided to come in and warm up. Annie was feeling tired and asked if she could go upstairs to lay down for a little while. After she left, Liam and I sat in the living room, watching a movie we had seen a hundred times. I watched as his face lit up every time the family was together and instantly felt bad that he didn't have that kind of childhood. I had been wanting to talk to him about how he felt about the new babies that were going to be joining our family soon, but we hadn't had much alone time and I didn't want to have that conversation with him in front of anyone else. I reached over and turned the volume down a little as I turned toward him on the couch.

"Hey, I've been meaning to ask you— how do you feel about all of the recent baby news?"

He looked over at me nervously, unsure of what to say. He shrugged and looked back at the tv.

"It's great, they're all going to be really happy with new babies."

"Liam, how do YOU feel about it? It's okay to be honest with me, you know that. There are no right or wrong answers."

"I don't know," he grumbled, irritated that he was having to talk to me about this. "I guess I'm fine with it, I'll have more cousins to play with. But really, I haven't thought about it that much."

"No? Why not?" I narrowed my eyes, knowing there was something else he wasn't telling me.

"I've been busy with other stuff," he said nonchalantly.

I arched a brow at him, wondering what he had been up to.

"You're on winter break and haven't left the house in a week- what could you possibly be busy with?" I asked with a chuckle.

"Protecting Annie." He turned to look at me as my stomach dropped.

"Protecting Annie from what?" I asked cautiously.

"From the monster that's coming for her."

For a moment I felt a bit of relief and wondered if Annie had nightmares like Lacey.

"Have you talked to her to tell her that monsters aren't real?" I pried softly.

"Yeah, but then I realized that she wasn't talking about fake monsters. She was talking about a real one."

My blood pressure started to rise as I realized that my son knew what was going on and hadn't bothered to tell me. If Lacey wasn't willing to talk to me, maybe I could get it out of Liam and prove to her that I could protect her against whatever monster was after them.

"Who is the real monster?" I asked sternly, forcing his attention back to me.

"She said she's not allowed to tell me, her mom said that if they talk about him, he'll find them. She was really scared after they ran away because there was so much fire in the house so she doesn't want him to know where they are because he'll try to take her mama away like he did her daddy." He paused for a moment as he thought about something. "But I think his name might be Bill."

"Why do you think that?"

"Because when we were playing outside earlier, she was using her stuffed puppy to fight off the bad guy and she kept saying- die, Bill, die! Then she said she didn't feel well and wanted to go to sleep."

I took in the information he had given me as I heard the garage door open, knowing that Lacey was back. I smiled and patted his knee as I got up, chuckling when I saw him reach for the remote to turn his movie back up after I left. I opened the door to the garage at the same time Lacey was reaching for it, forcing her to stumble in, directly into my arms.

She had shopping bags hanging from both arms and was wearing a new beanie that I hadn't seen before. She blew out a breath, forcing the stray piece of hair out of her face as she tried to regain her balance. I carefully slid the majority of the bags off of her arms and carried them into the kitchen, setting them on the table as she walked in behind me.

She pulled her gloves off as she glanced into the living room, looking for Annie. With concern on her face, she asked, "Where's Annie?"

"She said she was tired and asked to lay down, maybe 30 minutes ago," I replied as I helped her with the other bags.

"Was she okay?"

"I believe so, Liam said that she had said she wasn't feeling well. But in all fairness, he just told me that two minutes before you got here."

"Maybe I should go check on her," she said as she pulled her coat off and hung it on the back of the chair.

"Yeah, probably a good idea." I stayed watching her, unsure of whether I should tell her what Liam had told me. While I wanted to talk to her and get the truth, I didn't want Liam to know that I had ratted him out. I also needed to think through what he told me and decipher what was true, and what was being embellished by a child's imagination. A few awkward seconds passed without us saying anything before she turned and went upstairs to check on Annie.

I left her bags on the table since I didn't want to be disrespectful and go through the things she bought. Fifteen minutes later, she came into the kitchen with a look of concern etched on her face. I turned away from the stove, studying her as she shuffled through the bags on the counter.

"Everything okay?" I asked casually as I turned back to the stove and pushed the rest of the spaghetti noodles down into the boiling water.

"Yeah," she sighed. "I'm looking for my phone." She threw her hands up in the air as she stared at the bags with frustration. I dried my hands on the towel and flung it over my shoulder as I walked over to help her. I looked between the bags, seeing plenty of clothes and a few toys for Annie amongst a few bags of food. I watched her out of the corner of my eye as she started rummaging through the bags again, looking flustered.

I reached forward and grabbed the first bag I found, pulling items aside as I felt around for her phone. My fingers slid across something silky. Against my better judgment, I lifted a black, silk thong out of the bag, letting it hang off my finger as I studied it. I could feel the blood rush from my head, down to my groin, as I imagined Lacey wearing them. I slowly looked toward her at the same time she looked over, her skin turning red as she saw the underwear in my hand. We stayed staring at the underwear for what felt like minutes before I heard footsteps approaching the kitchen. Quickly, I shoved the panties back into the bag and pushed it down, trying to keep them hidden.

"Mommy, my head hurts," Annie whined from the doorway. I smiled at her and walked back to the stove, tending to the noodles before glancing over my shoulder to see if she needed help.

"I'm sorry, baby, I was looking for my phone, then I was going to get your Tylenol." Lacey sighed and stopped going through the bags to look at Annie.

"You left your phone on the dresser in the room. It keeps vibrating and beeping."

"No honey, mommy got a new phone today. That's the one I'm looking for." There was a worried look on Lacey's face as she said, pausing momentarily to look at Annie after she said that it had been vibrating. I turned around and kept my back turned to them, giving them as much privacy as I could while I wondered why she had gotten a new phone. There were a lot of unanswered questions that were making me doubt everything that I thought I knew about her.

"So, do I have to memorize this number now too?" Annie asked, sitting down at the table.

"No honey, this is just a temporary phone. You don't have to worry about any of that."

I felt Lacey's eyes on me as she said it. There was no way that I was going to be able to keep skirting around everything and acting like nothing was going on.

"Hey, Grant, do you have a thermometer?" Lacey asked as she held her hand to Annie's forehead.

"Yeah, let me grab it real quick." I set the fork on the counter as I walked over to the cabinet where I kept all of the medical stuff.

"Mommy, I don't feel well," Annie said right before she threw up all over the floor.

I rushed over and handed Lacey the thermometer before hurrying back to the sink and wetting a paper towel to give to Annie. Lacey took it and quickly cleaned Annie up before scanning her forehead with the thermometer. Her brows pulled together as she read the temperature, then scanned her again a few times just to be sure.

"What's she at?" I asked, knowing that Annie was running a fever higher than Lacey was comfortable with.

"103.5," she said warily.

"Do you want to try to get her to the hospital?" I knew that another storm was supposed to come through soon but I didn't doubt my ability to get her to the hospital if needed.

"I can watch her here for a little bit, see if I can get it to break or at least keep it from climbing. This came on pretty quickly so I'm not sure what we're looking at yet."

"What can I do to help?" I asked, hoping that she would let me.

"I don't want her too far from me, do you think she can rest on the couch?"

"Absolutely," I assured her as I worked with Liam to get everything cleaned up and set blankets and pillows out for her to lay down on. After Lacey got some Tylenol in her, she brought her in and laid her on the couch, tucking her in as she quickly went back to sleep.

I quickly cleaned up the kitchen while Lacey was checking on Annie, making sure there was nothing else for her to worry about. I finished the spaghetti and threw some garlic bread in the oven while I waited for Liam to wash up for dinner. Lacey cleared her bags from the table and set them in the living room before coming back to the kitchen.

"Dinner's ready," I said as she walked in. I nodded to the table where I had set out the spaghetti, salad, and bread. She smiled softly and looked up at me.

"Thank you," her voice was quiet but sincere.

"Don't thank me yet, it's spaghetti sauce from a jar," I joked.

"I'm sure it's delicious," she laughed as she took a seat. "But I meant thank you for helping me earlier. For watching Annie while I went to the store and for helping me with her being sick."

"It's no biggie." I shrugged my shoulders and smiled as I grabbed the Parmesan cheese shaker from the fridge and closed it. I could hear Liam in the bathroom washing his hands and knew I had a few minutes before he came in for dinner.

"So, who's Bill?" I asked as I sat down across from her. I watched as the color drained from her face as if she had just seen a ghost. She opened her mouth to say something at the same time Liam walked in and sat down. Her mouth quickly snapped shut as she excused herself and walked away.

Ten
Lacey

I felt bad for running off and not joining the guys for dinner but when Grant said Bill's name, my blood went ice cold and I had to get away. I had no idea what had happened while I was out at the store or what Annie might have told them. She was too little to really understand what was happening to begin with so I had to assume that anything she might have said could have been exaggerated, making things look worse than they were.

I leaned back against the couch after gently scanning her forehead again to check her fever. She was still at 103 which made me nervous that it wasn't dropping with the Tylenol. I had been applying cold washcloths to her head as well but even those weren't working. She was restless in her sleep, fighting some invisible demon that I couldn't help her with. I hated that she was sick, but I hated even more that I felt so helpless, not knowing how to help her. Usually, I would see when Annie was coming down with something and I could try to manage it head-on. This came out of nowhere and I was stumped, already feeling out of sorts with everything else going on.

An hour later I heard Liam go upstairs, the shower turning on a few minutes later. Grant quietly came into the living room holding a bowl of spaghetti with a piece of garlic bread laying on top. He smiled softly as he extended the bowl to me and said nothing. My stomach chose the worst time to growl, confirming that I was starving as I reached forward and took the bowl from him.

"Thank you," I said softly, trying to keep from disturbing Annie. He nodded in response before looking at Annie and raising his eyebrows to ask about her. "Still the same," I sighed as I glanced back at her. "I'm sorry, I was hoping to have already booked a hotel when I got back from the store so we would be out of your hair. I'll call soon and see if there are any vacancies."

"Lacey, you don't need to do that. You and Annie are fine here. Besides, it's not fair to her to try to move her around when she's this sick and needs rest. Just stay here, it's not a problem."

I smiled and let my shoulders relax as I twirled the noodles around my fork before taking a bite. Even though he said this was just sauce from a jar, it was still the best spaghetti I had eaten in a long time. I closed my eyes as I savored the flavor, allowing it to explode on my tongue. I shoved another bite into my mouth, quietly moaning as I did, lost in the delicious food before me. When I slowly opened my eyes, I found Grant sitting in the recliner, watching me intensely with his hands firmly gripping the end of the armrests. Subconsciously, I wiped my mouth with my finger, drawing more attention to my lips. I was about to look away when I heard footsteps approaching.

"I'm going to bed, Dad," Liam whispered as he waved to us before turning around and heading back upstairs.

"He's a good kid," I said softly, hoping to change the subject to anything other than the spaghetti foreplay we were just engaged in as I set the bowl on the coffee table beside me.

"Yeah, he really is."

"So, what all did Annie have to say earlier?" I asked knowing that we needed to talk about the elephant in the room. He pulled his eyebrows together in confusion as he had no idea what I was talking about.

"About Bill. What did she tell you?"

He leaned forward and blew out a heavy sigh.

"Annie didn't tell me anything. Liam did," he admitted.

"How did Liam know about him? How did this conversation even start?" I knew that Annie and Liam were spending a lot of time together playing but I didn't know that she was confiding our secrets in him as well.

"I had asked him how he felt about everyone having a new baby and he mentioned that he hadn't been focused on it too much because he was protecting Annie." His eyes searched mine as he said it, waiting for my facial expressions to give away my emotional reaction. I swallowed hard and looked away. I didn't want to ask the next question but I knew that I had to.

"Did he say what he's protecting her from?" I closed my eyes as I said it, bracing myself for what would come next. As I opened my eyes, I saw him nod yes and I felt the air rush out of my body. There was no way that we could stay here any longer now that he knew what I had done.

"He said that Annie is afraid of a monster named Bill."

Our eyes locked as my head whipped up at the sound of the name.

"I'm sorry, I didn't mean to put you in this position. We'll be gone by morning." I pulled in a deep breath, forcing the air back into my lungs as I sat a little taller and tried to pretend that I was stronger than I looked.

"Lacey, I still don't know what's happening, but I want to. I really, really, want to. I wish you would trust me enough to let me help you with whatever it is that you're running from."

"I can't tell you what happened, Grant. Can you please just trust me that I can handle this?" I begged as I glanced back at Annie.

"Do you really think that you can handle it? I'm not trying to be a dick but whatever it is seems to be pretty bad, and I know that when things get that bad, they are harder to handle on your own."

I looked down and nervously spun my wedding ring around my finger as I debated whether to tell him. I had felt alone for so long that it felt odd to have someone who not only wanted to be there for me, but they were begging me to let them help me. It was making my head cloudy and for a moment, I decided to give in and allow myself to trust again.

"Bill is my father." I looked up and saw the look on his face after I said it. He subtly nodded for me to go on. "After my husband died, I didn't have a choice but to move back home and live with him until I could get on my feet again. I was working full time and 12-hour shifts meant that I wasn't home when I needed to get Annie to and from school. Or to get dinner on the table. I was so used to Derek picking up the slack and the teamwork that made everything run so smoothly between us. When he died, the first thing that I thought was – how am I going to do this on my own?" I let out a ragged breath as my fingers trembled in response.

"So I moved back home with my father because I didn't have any other options. I was so overwhelmed with grief. Having our lives completely uprooted and changed in one day (or overnight), I subconsciously blocked out everything from my childhood. Those are the terrible memories turned nightmares that still haunt me."

Grant's eyes never left mine as he listened quietly to every word that I said.

"My dad was a bad man. IS a bad man. A raging alcoholic with a passion for beating women when they don't do as he says. I watched him beat my mom every day growing up until the day he killed her. I was seven when it happened and I can still remember every single detail about that day. When the cops showed up, he told them that she had fallen and hit her head on the edge of the counter. I didn't want to lie to them but he had already promised me that they would take me away if I told them the truth and that they would put me in a home with people who would do worse things. I was used to my dad beating me as it was, I couldn't imagine living somewhere where someone else would treat me worse than that. So, I lied and pretended that I didn't know what had happened. No one gives that much credit to a child that age so they didn't bother pressing me for more information."

"Shortly after I had moved back, I noticed he had started drinking again. Derek and I didn't visit him often and he had only met Annie a handful of times. We lived in Montana and he was still back in Colorado, so distance was a good excuse not to visit. When Derek died, he made an effort to come to the funeral to show his support. He was sober for once and had told me that he had been sober for fifteen years. I was at my absolute worst- a widow with a young child and no one to turn to. When he wanted to act like a dad and show me the kind of love that I had always wanted, I jumped at the opportunity. He made it sound so perfect when he talked about how he was going to help me with Annie and be the grandpa she deserved."

I felt movement behind me and turned to look at Annie. She was still asleep but restless as she turned over and tried to get comfortable. I continued talking, lowering my voice as I scooted closer to Grant so he could still hear me.

"We hadn't been there long when I started noticing that he was drinking. Not just a drink here and there- he was drunk all day long. It started bringing back old childhood memories so I started to panic, wondering if I had made a big mistake moving back home and subjecting my daughter to this environment." I let out a breath and took a moment to collect myself before I continued.
"One day he was pissed because I had burned dinner. But the problem was that he thought I was my mom. He started yelling and calling me

by her name before he tried to attack me. Annie saw it and cowered in the corner, terrified. When he saw her, he thought she was me. Somehow he was transported back in time in his drunken stupor that he thought it was my mother he was beating and his daughter who was watching. After that he started to get obsessed with Annie – not in a gross way—but in a 'frustrated that she didn't love him like she should love a grandfather' kind of way. His drinking was out of control. I was terrified to leave the house and have Annie there by herself."

I watched as Grant's jaw moved back and forth as he listened, anger and irritation evident on his face.

"So I decided we needed to leave. I packed a few bags and hid them in my car, just in case. One afternoon, he was hellbent on picking a fight and I didn't have it in me. He pinned me to the wall by my throat and told me all of the hateful things he had wanted to say since I was a child. This time he knew who I was and he knew who Annie was. I gasped for air as Annie came up and hit him in the back with the baseball bat that he keeps by the front door. It was enough for him to drop me and for me to catch my breath, but I knew that it was the breaking point that I needed to force us to get out of there. Long story short, there was a scuffle and I was trying to get Annie out. I told her to run and as she did, he kicked the coffee table and shot it out toward her, tripping her and causing her to fall and hit her face on the edge of it. That's how she got the bruise. Annie was able to get out and go to the car like I asked her to."

My lip trembled as I struggled to keep going, to confess the sin I had committed.

"He tried to go after Annie so I lunged forward and knocked him to the ground. It didn't take long until he was on top of me and trying to choke me. I was already pretty weak from the other attacks so I knew I wasn't going to be able to fight him off. Instead, I laid there and played dead. He got up a few minutes later and went looking for Annie. Knowing that I didn't have any other choice, I grabbed the baseball bat and hit him in the head with it, hard enough to knock him to the floor." A single tear slid down my cheek as Grant's thumb gently reached over and wiped it away. "I ran to the shed and grabbed a can of gasoline and a pack of matches. When I went back into the house I was relieved to see him still lying there. I was furious with him for so many things that I didn't think about it as I poured the gas all over the carpet and lit a match. The house was engulfed in flames by the time I got to the car with Annie. Once I saw that she was safe and he wasn't around, I threw the car in drive and sped off. I got the hell out of there and didn't look back."

He continued to listen, complete empathy on his face as he took in the words that felt like razors coming out of my mouth.

"The past few days I had been hopeful that he had died in the fire. That he hadn't come to and been able to get out in time. I hadn't heard from him so what else could I think?" A sob escaped my throat as I tried to force myself to keep going. "But then this morning I had 3 missed calls from him and they haven't stopped since then. I haven't listened to all of the voicemails yet, but the ones I did listen to were pretty detailed in how he wanted to make me pay for what I did."

I closed my eyes as more tears slid down my face. Nightmares of what I had done haunted me every night since it happened but in each dream, I knew where he was. I knew that I had won and that he would never be able to hurt us again. I shook my head to try to get rid of the images as I buried my head in my hands and cried silently, the way I learned to cry after Derek died. Grant reached forward and gently pulled me, bringing me up to sit with him as he wrapped his arms around me and held me as we rocked gently.

"Is that where you were coming from the night of the accident?" he asked quietly. I shook my head yes.

"Where does your dad live?"

"Easterville, it's a small town a few hours away from here."
"I've heard of it but I've never been there."

"You're not missing out on anything," I joked between muffled sobs.

"You're a very brave woman, Lacey," he said as he softly placed a finger under my chin and turned my face to look at him.

"I'm not brave. I'm stupid. I never should have moved in with him, and I never should have left without making sure he couldn't come after us."

"You're safe here, I promise you that. I will not let anything happen to either of you." His tone was soft as he held me tighter when he said it.

"Thank you, I appreciate that. But we can't stay here. He'll find us. And if he finds us, he'll kill us." I felt the sharp breath that Grant took when he heard my words and knew that we needed to leave before things got even more complicated than they already were.

Eleven
Grant

The next couple of days were rough as Annie got worse before she got better. I tried staying out of Lacey's way and minding my own business, but as a father, it was hard to look the other way when it was so obvious that Annie needed medical attention. Lacey grew as frustrated with me as I was with her which created this thick tension around us.

I had tried to talk to her about what she had told me about her father the other night but she constantly avoided it and would instantly change the subject. She was, by far, the most infuriating woman I had ever met. Sexy as hell—but she had a way of getting under my skin without trying. It was Friday night and Liam and I had planned to do pizza and a few movies to wrap up the end of his winter break before he started back to school on Monday. As I went by his room, I glanced in and saw Lacey packing their duffle bags with the clean laundry she had just pulled out of the dryer.

"What are you doing?" I asked as I leaned against the doorway and folded my arms over my chest.

"Packing," she sighed, not bothering to look at me.

"Where are you going?" I knew my tone had changed and the frustration was evident but I didn't give a damn.

"I was able to book a room at the inn down the street for a few nights." She folded a pair of sweatpants and shoved them down into the bag that was already packed to the brim. I blew out a frustrated breath and ran a hand through my hair.

"What's this all about? Really?" I asked as calmly as I could.

"We've been here a week, it's time for us to get out of your hair and let you get back to your lives."

I pushed off from the wall and walked over, putting my hand over the top of the bag so she couldn't stuff anything else inside.

"Did I ask you to go? Have I insinuated that you and Annie haven't been welcome here or that it's been an inconvenience for us?"

"No," she sighed and turned to look at me, dropping the shirt in her hand onto the bed. "But that doesn't mean that we should outstay our welcome. This was never in the plan…"

"You admitted yourself that there was no plan other than getting out of that house and finding somewhere to go that was safe. If you ask me— you've accomplished that plan."

She eyed me cautiously as if she was waiting for me to change my mind and tell her to get her things and get packing.

"Do you have a new plan? Any idea where you're going to go? How you're going to get by until you get settled in? You said it yourself that you moved in with your dad because you needed help getting back on your feet after Derek died. What makes you think that you're going to get on your feet by leaving and running off on your own again?" I knew my words probably sounded harsh but I needed her to think things through and to realize that she didn't have anything set up for her and Annie. It was completely reckless to just take off and not have any idea where they were going or what she was going to do. Who was going to look after Annie while she worked? There were so many things that I was worried about and it completely surprised me that Lacey wasn't concerned about anything other than getting out of my house.

"No, but that's not the point. You didn't ask for any of this, Grant. It's not fair to you that we came storming in and completely shifted everything in your life." Her face fell when she said it, realizing what she was saying. She closed her eyes and shook her head before looking back at me. "I'm sorry, I didn't mean for it to come out that way," she apologized.

"It's fine. The truth is that we do know what it's like to have everything shift and have our lives turned upside down. It's not fair, but at least this time it brought two new people into our lives instead of taking someone away." I smiled sympathetically, hoping to ease some of the discomfort I could still see on her face.

"I don't know what to do. What am I supposed to do?" She threw her hands up in the air and plopped down on the bed. The look in her eyes told me that she was genuinely asking.

"What do you want to do?"

"I want to stop running and find somewhere safe for Annie to grow up. Somewhere that doesn't remind her of everything that she's lost. Somewhere we can just slow down for a bit and not always be rushing for something." She let out a heavy sigh as her shoulders slumped, the stress of the week starting to show in how tired she looked.

"Then stay here and let me help you," I offered. My pulse started racing as I panicked about what I was saying. I knew deep down that I meant it, I really wanted to help her. But this was all new territory for me and I was terrified that I wouldn't know how to handle it. The thought of living with a woman and her child, permanently, scared the shit out of me. Knowing that she had nowhere else to go and was safer here with me, where I could protect them, was the only thing that kept me from turning around and leaving a giant hole in the wall as I burst through it like the Kool-Aid man.

She nervously chewed her bottom lip as she thought about it.

"We need to agree on certain conditions first," she said and I tried not to roll my eyes as I chuckled. Of course, this damn woman would have conditions.

"Okay, let's hear them." I took a step back and spread my feet apart as I crossed my arms over my chest and stared at her.

"First- there won't be any more of you catering to us. We will help with the chores around the house, including cooking and cleaning." She arched an eyebrow and waited before I rolled my eyes and nodded yes.

"Second- I will start contributing to the monthly bills including paying rent and splitting the cost of the utilities. I have some money still saved up from selling the house in Montana, however, I plan to start looking for a job immediately."

I clenched my jaw as I listened. There was no way in hell that I was going to let her pay half of the bills that I was already used to paying. That money should be set aside for an emergency, or a college fund for Annie. She was out of her mind if she thought I was going to take it. I stayed quiet and let her continue before I countered with my own conditions.

"Third- I know that there may be times when you will need to look after Annie for me, and maybe I can help watch Liam for you. Can we please agree to be respectful of each other's parenting styles and not undo everything that we have in place? Change can be hard for kids so it's important that you and I stay united on this one." She looked at me with a desperation in her eyes that said this wasn't the first time she's had to have this conversation with someone.

"What else?" I asked, unsure of whether she had more conditions. She pursed her lips and squinted her eyes as she looked at the wall, concentrating, before turning back to look at me and smiling.

"That's it I think. But of course, there's always the standing option to modify or add any additional conditions later on as we see fit," she said playfully with a smirk on her face.

"Fair enough," I chuckled. "Okay, here's my counter to your conditions. I will try to budge and let you help out with some of the chores. Since you're a better cook, maybe you can do more of the cooking and I'll do all of the cleaning?" I laughed as she frowned and folded her arms over her chest.

"Okay, fine. We'll consider keeping it 50/50. For now. Second- you will not pay half of the bills or utilities. I've been paying them just fine on my own, so while I appreciate the offer, I respectfully decline. Save that money and use it for an emergency fund, or keep it for Annie if she wants to go to college." I took a deep breath and let my arms relax as I looked at her. "Third- I will never question your parenting with Annie, nor would I ever try to undo anything that you've done. I can't imagine how I would feel if someone did that to me, so I won't do that to you."

She smiled and mouthed thank you as if it was something special that I was doing for her.

"I have some conditions of my own when you're ready." I winked and waited for her blush to finish creeping up her fair skin.

"Let's hear them," she said and scooted back on the bed.

"First, this isn't a temporary thing. You and Annie will stay with me for as long as you need until you're ready to go. It can be a few months or it can be a few years- I don't care. But for the love of God, please stop trying to book a hotel room. You're driving me crazy with that. If you book another room- it better be because you want some alone time and have something special planned for yourself." I paused when I noticed the blush creeping her cheeks again. I licked my lips, wondering what could possibly be going through her mind that would have her reacting this way.

"While we're on the topic of you and Annie living here, I think we need to discuss making this place more functional. You can't keep sleeping in this tiny ass bed with Annie, and I can't keep getting kicked in the ribs by Liam every time he thinks I'm going to snore," I joked.

"Okay, what do you suggest?"

"I want to go shopping and if you're okay with it, I suggest converting Liam's room to a space that he and Annie can share. I know it's a small room, but I think if we get creative enough, we can make it work."

I watched as panic rushed across her face as she listened.

"Grant, no, there's no need to do that."

"Lacey, you agreed to stay with me and to let me help you get on your feet. So yeah, there is a need. Annie needs to be able to feel like she has a home, she can't live out of that duffel bag forever."

She rubbed her lips together and tapped her foot on the carpet. I could tell that this was hard for her to accept and I wanted to make it as easy for her as possible.

"Trust me, it will be fun and Annie will love getting to pick out her own bed and dresser," I said calmly, hoping to ease some of her anxiety. "I'll help Liam clean up his room and we'll pack up some of the stuff he doesn't play with anymore and move it up to the attic. There's plenty of room in here for two standard beds and two dressers. They can share the space in the closet, and I'll add another bar along the lower half, giving them more room."

"Fine," she said reluctantly. "Annie can share a room with Liam. I'll sleep on the couch and keep my stuff out of the way."

My eyebrows shot up high on my forehead as I heard what she was planning. Did she really think that she was going to live here and sleep on the couch every night?

"Yeah, I don't think so. You'll move into my room with me." I felt my breath hitch as I said it. It was a huge leap for me but I kept reminding myself that it wasn't anything romantic, it was simply a living arrangement that revolved around a house that was now too small for the four people who were trying to live in it.

"There's no way that I can do that. It wouldn't be appropriate, what would the kids think?" she shrieked, eyes wide in horror.

"They'll think that we're trying to make everyone as comfortable as possible with our new living situation in a small house. My room is plenty big enough, and if it makes you feel more comfortable, I can get rid of my bed and we can get two full-sized beds instead." I waited anxiously for her to respond.

She finally let out the breath she was holding and looked me in the eyes, holding my stare.

"So I get stuck with the snorer?"

I watched as the smile spread across her face before she erupted in laughter, falling back on the pillows as I reached forward and playfully swatted her leg.

"Just for that, you don't get a separate bed," I teased, secretly hoping that she wouldn't want to go through with separate beds after all. It would be strange having a woman in my bed again, and I knew it would be hard to get used to, but I honestly really loved my bed and wasn't ready to part with it.

"Alright, I think we agree on all conditions, however, I do have one more." She stood up and stepped close enough to me that I could smell the vanilla from her shower gel. "I get to buy the furniture for Annie, and if Liam gets excited that she's getting new furniture, then I'll buy him new stuff too."

Before I could open my mouth to protest she lifted a finger and placed it on my lips.

"I would be spending this money either way once I found a place for Annie and me to live. I won't argue this with you so please stop acting like a damn cock in a hen house and just agree to this." She pinned me with a look that made me want to do everything she asked and more.

"Fine," I sighed and shrugged my shoulders.

"Good, I'm glad we have that situated." She smiled smugly.

"You're impossible, you know that?" I stepped a fraction of a hair closer, my eyes searching hers for any indication that she wasn't feeling as hot and bothered as I was by being this close to each other. Her lips slightly parted as she leaned forward, gently reaching out and holding onto my shoulder as she leaned in close to my ear.

"So I've been told," she whispered as she pulled back and walked away, allowing her hand to drop and brush across my stomach in the process.

There was no doubt about it—this woman was going to be the death of me.

68

Twelve
Lacey

Saturday morning came quickly as we got up early to get a head start on shopping before Grant and Liam had to go to Rylee's first birthday party that afternoon. We sat down with the kids at breakfast and explained the new living situation, including them sharing a room. I was relieved when they both had grins stretching from ear to ear as they excitedly talked about their plans for their new room. Grant and I sat back and listened, both in awe of how well they got along. Almost like brother and sister.

It killed me that Annie didn't have any siblings to share these experiences with, so it was bittersweet that she had Liam and he had her. Both of them were dealt a real shitty card in life with losing a parent and I could relate to how lonely it could be as an only child. I always wanted to give Annie a sibling but Derek and I had the hardest time conceiving her that I knew it would be harder to try to have another one. You have to want to have sex in order to get pregnant and Derek was rarely in the mood after we had Annie.

We cleaned up and hopped in the truck for the first time as a make-shift family of four. I smiled as I sat in the passenger seat and glanced behind me to see Annie and Liam sitting next to each other, excitement on their faces as we made our way to the store. Excitement flooded through me as I imagined this being our new life, going places together as a family, then I remembered that it wasn't really like that. It was a living arrangement that was as temporary as we wanted it to be.

Once inside the store, the kids ran ahead to the back of the store so they could start checking out the bed options for Annie. Liam had confirmed that he didn't want a new bed, he loved the one he had. Grant had recently purchased him a new bed when they moved out of his mother's house, shortly after Renee had passed. It was the first big purchase they had made after being on their own and was special to both of them.

I pushed a shopping cart alongside Grant as we followed the kids, knowing that I needed to get more stuff for Annie than just furniture. If we were going to actually live there, she needed more of her own stuff. Including some toys and new clothes for school. I had no idea what the plan was for her going to school and figured now was as good of a time as any to ask Grant about Liam's school.

"Hey, I was wondering, do you think Annie would be able to start school on Monday with Liam? Or am I way too late to get her registered?" I worried my lip in between my teeth as I realized how much there was to get done.

"I'm sure they can get her in. I'll make a call later and talk to the principal, let her know what's going on."

"You know the principal that well that you can just call them up and ask for a favor?" I asked suspiciously.

"Yeah, I know the principal that well. She's an old friend, and she happens to be my boss."

"You work at the school?" I turned my head to look at him as we rounded a corner and almost caught up to the kids.

"Yeah, I teach P.E." He shrugged as he walked over to where the kids were standing and looking at a white daybed with pink roses that ran along the arch of the frame.

"I can't believe I didn't know what you did," I said more to myself than to him. "I'm sorry, I feel so rude that I didn't think to ask before."

"Well it hasn't really come up in conversation," he laughed as he turned to look at me. "I'll call Mary and ask her if you can go by Monday morning to get Annie registered. We can grab some basic supplies today too, that way she'll have everything she needs."

His smile was so sweet and genuine that I found myself smiling back and honestly believing that everything would work out.

Hundreds of dollars later the shopping cart was filled to the top with new clothes and school supplies for Annie, along with the new furniture she had picked out that was in the cart that Grant was pushing. I reached down and checked my cell phone, making sure we were doing okay on time so they didn't miss the party. There were a few things that I had wanted to look at getting for myself but didn't want to tie up anyone's day longer than needed. As I was about to slide my cell phone back into my pocket, I felt it vibrate with a new call. Trying to be as discrete as possible, I glanced at the caller ID and felt relieved when it wasn't my dad. I could feel Grant's eyes watching me as I debated whether to answer the call or not.

"I need to take this call real quick," I said quietly, so only Grant could hear me. He nodded as he pushed the cart the other way, taking the kids with him to go look around, giving me some privacy. I sucked in a deep breath as I slid my finger across the screen to answer it.

"Hey," I said in a half-whisper as my voice started to break.

"Lacey Ann Holbrook – where the hell are you and are you and Annie okay?!"

I pulled the phone back from my ear to get away from the loud shriek that greeted me on the other side.

"Are you by yourself?" I asked as my voice evened out some as I turned my cart and wandered down the lotion and body wash aisle. Kayce was my cousin and best friend growing up, the only person that I've ever been close with, and knew all of the dark secrets of my family, never judging me for any of it.

"Yes, I am by myself. I just got back into town and heard about the fire from my mom," she sighed heavily. "Tell me the truth Lacey, are you guys okay? Are you safe?"

"We are okay and we are safe. But I can't tell you where we're at and I can't talk about what happened," I explained knowing that she would already know and understand why. I looked around at the different body washes and grabbed one with a tropical-looking label on it. Hawaiian Paradise. I smiled softly as I let myself fantasize about how wonderful that sounded as I tossed a bottle of it into my cart.

"Okay, that's all I need to know. I won't ask for details, I know better."

"Thank you, I appreciate that," I said as I slowly moved the cart forward and tossed in a few more items including some mud face masks and a couple of bath bombs. I wasn't even sure that Grant had a bathtub in his house, the only bathrooms I had been in were either a half bath or was limited to a walk-in shower. I shrugged and left them in the cart as I kept walking.

"You know, if you would have moved in with me you wouldn't have had to worry about this in the first place, you know?" she teased, forcing a smile across my face.

"Oh please, Kayce, you barely even fit in your studio apartment! There's no way that Annie and I would have fit there," I laughed and shook my head at the thought. "Plus, you're never home anymore, living the glamorous life of constantly being on the road with the hottest rock star on the west coast. How's that going by the way?" I asked, hoping to change the subject.

I suddenly remembered a few other things that I needed so I turned and headed in that direction, making sure that I stayed mindful of the time so I didn't make Grant and Liam late for the birthday party.

"It's okay I guess. I don't see him much when I travel with him so I don't know why I go anymore. They're constantly practicing or having band only meetings so I just end up sitting alone in the hotel or I go sightseeing on my own. It's getting kind of boring."

"That sucks," I said as I listened and shopped at the same time. "I guess it's never as glamorous as it seems, is it?"

"Not at all. I just got back this morning and decided to stay here and skip the next few stops they were going on. I'm tired and really wanted to just be home for a while. But then I got back and found out about you and Annie which made me feel terrible that I wasn't here to begin with."

"Honestly, there wasn't anything that you could have done. If you were there it would have just put you in danger and I would never want that."

"I know, but I hate that now you're on the run and I might not ever get to see you guys again."

"If I didn't run, you most likely wouldn't see us again anyways," I said softly as a somber tone fell between us.

"I know. For what it's worth, I wish you had been dealt a better card in life than having Bill as a father."

"Me too, kiddo, me too."

Kayce was only two years younger than me but I always felt like her big sister growing up. I settled down at an early age, got married, and had a baby all before I was 21. She just turned 25 and was traveling with her rock star boyfriend, seeing the world with very few responsibilities to tie her down. Her last big expense was the dragon tattoo she got on her back as a birthday present to herself after coloring her hair bright pink. She worked as a mechanic in Easterville which didn't pay much but kept her afloat with what she wanted to do with her life.

A few minutes later we said our goodbyes as I spotted Grant and started making my way toward them. Kayce promised to keep in touch and to let me know if she heard anything more about my dad. She hadn't bothered trying to get any information on him before she called so she knew as much about his whereabouts as I did. I felt a tad bit uneasy that I was talking to her, knowing that he could go after her at any time, trying to get information out of her. I pulled my cart up alongside Grant's and smiled as the kids came up beside him.

"I think we're all set. We can go check out so we have time to get everything home in time for you and Liam to get over to the birthday party," I said as I started to turn my cart toward the check-out line. Grant's brows pulled together as he adjusted his cart to follow mine.

"You're not coming with us?" he asked with a hint of disappointment in his tone.

"Why would we? It's your family." I was genuinely confused as to why he would assume that we were going.

"So? You've met everyone. You spent hours talking to them on New Year's Eve. They expect that you and Annie will be there with us today."

I watched as Annie's face turned up to look at me, her brown curls bouncing down her back.

"Can we go, mommy? Pllleeeasssee?" she whined as she held her hands together and begged me. I glanced at Grant out of the corner of my eye and saw the smirk on his face knowing that I wouldn't be able to say no to her.

"Okay, fine. We'll go," I sighed, shooting a glare his way. "But we need to get her a present and a card before we go."

"You can share ours," Grant offered before I shot him down with another look.

"We are not showing up to a birthday party without a card and a gift of our own," I warned as I turned my cart around, almost knocking myself and the cart over as it struggled with the weight in it. I heard Grant laugh behind me as I made my way back to the toy section.

The day felt long as we rushed home and unloaded everything from the truck into the living room before packing up Rylee's gifts and rushing out of the house again. Thankfully they only lived a few minutes away so we weren't as late as I had expected we would be. Grant held the door open as Liam rushed in, letting Annie and I go in next. I could feel my palms start to sweat as I looked around and instantly felt out of place with Grant's family. There were a few people that I knew but a handful of people that I hadn't met yet. Curious eyes started making their way toward us as I heard a few whispers of people asking who we were.

A few seconds later I smiled as I saw Mia come rushing over, quickly grabbing me and pulling me in for a hug. Grant wasn't lying when he said that she was one of the nicest people he knew.

"Lacey! I'm so glad that you and Annie could make it today!" she said excitedly as she pulled back and smiled at me before looking down to say hi to Annie. "I can take that," she offered as she reached for the gift bag and set it on the table behind us before leading me off to meet everyone else.

Everyone was just as friendly as Mia and apparently super curious about why Grant was there with a woman. Were they dating? Did they know each other long? Was it true that she was living with him? I tried to ignore the whispers as I made my way to the kitchen to see if I could help out with anything while Annie ran off with Liam to go play with Rylee.

The kitchen was tied into the living room as it all flowed into one which didn't really allow for a place to hide, which was what I was needing. I found Jade by the sink with her back turned toward everyone as she sliced a tomato and set it to the side. She grabbed another one and went to slice it when her hand slipped and I watched in slow motion as the knife went directly into her hand. A slew of curse words came flying out of her mouth as the knife fell to the sink before she quickly turned and held her hand away from the food as blood starting trickling down her hand. In an instant Noah was by her side, grabbing a paper towel and wrapping her hand as it quickly turned bright red from the blood.

"Are you okay?" Mia asked panicky as she came rushing over to see what had happened.

"Yeah, I missed and cut myself instead of the damn tomato," Jade grunted as Noah tried to hold the paper towel that was now soaked in blood against her hand. I could tell by the look of it that she was going to need help to get the bleeding under control.

"I can help with that," I offered, feeling my cheeks heat as everyone stopped and turned to look at me. "I'm a trauma nurse in the ER," I explained.

A few minutes later I helped Jade sit down, making sure the toilet seat lid was down first, and waited for Mia to bring the first aid kit they had. I smiled as I took it from her, watching as Jade held her hand over the sink as it continued to bleed.

"Will I need stitches?" Jade asked, looking up at me.

"I'm not sure yet, but hopefully not. I'll see what I can do to stop the bleeding first."

"Noah is going to give me crap about this," she muttered under her breath as Mia watched from the doorway. I opened the first aid kit that Mia had brought and prayed that it had the supplies I would need. I was relieved when I looked inside and found a decent supply of bandages and tape. Quickly I set the items that I needed out on the counter beside the sink and gently reached over to check on Jade's hand.

"Why's that?" I asked as I slowly pulled the paper towel away, being careful to not go too fast and risk opening the wound again. I took a closer look and was pleased to see that the bleeding had started to slow down which was a good sign.

"Because he's scared of everything. He would wrap me in bubble wrap and lock me in the house if he thought it would keep me safe." She rolled her eyes and shook her head as she and Mia shared a private look in the mirror.

"Some men get like that when their partner is pregnant," I laughed and quickly worked to get the paper towel off before it started bleeding heavily again.

"Yeah, I'm sure. He's just afraid because this is our miracle baby." She looked up and locked eyes with me as I glanced at her.

"Miracle baby?" I tilted my head to the side to glance at her before I turned my attention back to focus on getting a new bandage in place.

"I lost a baby, almost a year ago." There was a sadness in her voice that broke my heart. That was a loss that I was familiar with as well, even though nobody knew. Not even Derek.

"I'm so sorry for your loss." I smiled down at her as I continued to wrap another bandage around her hand, just to make sure.

"Thank you. I was around 8 weeks when it happened, but I didn't know that I was pregnant. We didn't think that I would or *could* get pregnant again, so this one was a big surprise."

"That's wonderful, how far along are you?" I asked as I cut the tape and gently pushed it down to make sure it was going to hold. I gathered up the supplies and started putting them back in the kit.

"I'll be 14 weeks tomorrow. Mia and I are basically having twins, she's 13 weeks as of yesterday." They smiled at each other in the mirror and I felt a sting of jealousy as I admired their friendship and this wonderful journey that they would get to share together.

"Alright, I think you're all set," I said as I stepped back and looked down at her hand. "We'll keep an eye on it just to make sure it doesn't start bleeding again, but I don't think you're going to need stitches."

I smiled as she thanked me before I ducked out of the room and went to find Grant. I walked down the hallway with my head down, not paying attention when I almost crashed into someone. I quickly looked up and saw a younger version of Grant smiling down at me.

"I'm so sorry," I said as I tried to excuse myself, turning awkwardly so I was walking backwards to the living room behind me.

"So you must be the hot new girl who's shacking up with my brother?" He said as he stepped to the side and watched me. I stopped in my tracks, unsure of what to say as I felt Grant come up behind me. I didn't have to hear his voice to know he was there. My body told me by the tingles that radiated through it every time he was around.

"Really, Wyatt?" he sighed as he placed his hand on my lower back possessively.

"What?" He shrugged. "She is hot, they weren't lying."

I felt my body turn fifty shades of red from embarrassment before the thought hit me that someone had been talking about me and it had gotten back to Grant's brother. And if someone knew that I was new in town, that meant that I wasn't going to be able to lay low after all. I looked up at Grant with worry on my face as I thought about amending our conditions and getting the hell out of town.

78

Thirteen
Grant

Lacey was quiet on the ride back from Chase's house and the kids were worn out in the back. I knew that it had been a long, overwhelming day for everyone, but something was different with Lacey and I couldn't quite put my finger on it. Part of me wondered if it was the phone call she had taken while we were at the store. As I pulled into the garage, I saw Annie and Liam undo their seatbelts, excited to go inside and get everything set up for their new room. I glanced at Lacey and saw the exhaustion on her face and knew everything would have to wait until tomorrow.

"Hey dad, can we go build Annie's bed so we can sleep in our new room together tonight?" Liam asked excitedly as he waited behind me as I opened the door into the house.

"It's late, son, and there's a lot that goes into building furniture. How about we do it first thing in the morning instead?" I offered, hoping he wouldn't be too disappointed.

"Yeah, I guess that's fine." He patted me on the back before saying goodnight to Lacey and Annie and running upstairs to get ready for bed. I was relieved that I didn't need to bug him to do it tonight.

"I'm tired too, mama," Annie said as she tugged at Lacey's sweater.

"Okay, honey, why don't you go get ready for bed too. I'll be up in just a minute." Lacey ran her hand through Annie's hair, pushing it out of her eyes before she ran upstairs to do as her mom asked.

I waited a few seconds until the kids were upstairs before talking to Lacey about what was bothering her. She looked exhausted so I didn't want to keep her up too long, but I wanted to make sure she wasn't going to have another hotel room booked by morning. She slid out of her jacket and hung it over the back of the chair in the kitchen before turning to look at me.

"I think I'm going to head upstairs and call it a night too," she said with a tired smile as she tried to fight off a yawn.

"Real quick, before you go," I reached out and gently grabbed her arm, pulling her back into the kitchen before she walked away. "I just wanted to make sure you're okay. You seemed upset when Wyatt was talking to you. Which I get, he tends to have that effect on people," I joked, hoping to lighten the mood.

"I'm okay, just nervous that Wyatt heard about me staying with you through the grapevine. I was hoping to find someplace where we could lay low but I know that's almost impossible in small towns."

"I get it, I really do. But I wouldn't worry too much about what Wyatt knows. If there's a new woman anywhere in a 50-foot radius he can find her. I swear he's going to get himself in trouble someday with all of the women he messes around with," I chuckled. "We used to think that Noah was bad until he settled down with Jade. After that, Wyatt took his place and has been unstoppable ever since."

"Maybe he just needs to find a girl who can settle him down, as Jade did with Noah," she teased.

"I don't think there's a single girl in Haven Brook that can tame him. He needs someone who won't put up with his shit and will put him in his place."

"Sounds like a challenge for my cousin, Kayce, they don't call her a man-eater for nothing." She laughed and I could hear that it was forced nervous laughter.

"You sure you're okay? Am I going to wake up to you packing to go to the hotel again in the morning?"

"No," she laughed. "We made a deal, I'll stick to it. Besides, I'm too tired to call and make a reservation."

I laughed at her joke, earning a cute smile from her in return. We said goodnight as she wandered upstairs. My mind had been busy all day as I struggled to figure out what all of these changes meant. Earlier at the birthday party, while Lacey was helping Jade with her cut, my mom cornered me to ask about Lacey and whether we were a thing. Everyone was thinking the same thing, drawing the same conclusions, but no one wanted to ask me about it.

Part of me wondered what life would be like if Lacey and Annie stayed with us forever. Would we continue to feel like the family we felt like earlier when we were at the store? Would we continue to share meals together and ask about each other's days? Everything felt so simple now, I wondered what it would be like the longer we went on pretending this was something it wasn't. I gave up trying to clear my head and went upstairs to try to get some rest, relieved that tonight would hopefully be the last night of getting kicked in my ribs every time I started to snore. If the kids thought they were excited about the new room arrangements, they had no idea how excited I was about it.

82

Fourteen
Lacey

I cowered in the corner of the room, under the kitchen table as I watched my dad stand over my mom, his knuckles white from how hard his hands were wrapped around her throat. She looked panicked as she tried to move out from underneath him, her arms swinging in the air as she tried to make contact with him. I could see her losing the battle, I could see the life draining from her body. In the last few seconds, her head turned toward me and her eyes locked onto mine. There was nothing but love and sadness behind them as I watched her fade away.

I screamed inside, desperate to help her. Desperate to bring her back to life. I knew that if I made any noise, I would be next. My dad grunted as he stood up and kicked her, grabbing his open beer off the counter and stumbled into the living room. I wrapped my arms around my knees as I stared at her and cried silently, wishing for one last hug. One last moment to tell her how much I loved her. I closed my eyes and pictured us sitting outside on a blanket, having a picnic while we looked up at the sky and made up stories about the images we found in the shapes of the cloud.

All of that was gone now. I was all by myself, left to learn how to protect myself from the only person I had left. The person who was supposed to love me but had constantly told my mom that she should have had the abortion when he told her to. My life would never be the same and I knew that. He had robbed me of everything that I had ever wanted and needed. To be loved.

I felt the wetness on my face as the tears slid down my cheeks, slowly waking me from the nightmare. I was desperate to wake up, to escape from the memory, but my mind and body were too exhausted to let me. Off in the distance, I could hear voices. Faint voices that sounded familiar. I struggled to listen as my dream shifted to one of Derek. It was the day of our wedding, the first time I had really been happy since before my mom died. I remembered smiling as I watched all of the guests start to arrive from the room where I was getting ready. Then came the moment of dread when I saw my father get out of his car and walk into the church as if he belonged there.

The voices got louder, an urgency to them. A fear. He wasn't supposed to be there. He wasn't invited. Panic filled me as I recognized the voice. It was Annie's voice. None of this made sense, Annie wasn't at our wedding. So who was she talking to? I felt my blood run cold when I realized that I wasn't hearing her in my dream, she was talking to someone right beside me. My eyelids felt heavy as I desperately tried to open them, forcing my body to wake up. There was a male's voice that I could hear now too but it sounded further away. I pushed harder, wishing someone would shake me and make my body do what I needed it to.

"I'll see you later, grandpa," Annie's voice was soft as my eyes blinked rapidly as I woke up. A movement from the corner of my eye forced my head to whip in the direction of the door as I saw a shadow move in the hallway. I quickly glanced at Annie as she rolled over and curled into her stuffed puppy before she let out a breath confirming she was asleep.

My body was shaking as I replayed her words over and over in my head as I slowly got out of bed and looked for something to use as a weapon. Liam's room was filled with toys but none of which looked like a promising weapon to use against someone lurking in the shadows. Knowing that I didn't have much time, I reached down and grabbed the first thing that my hand came in contact with while keeping an eye on the door.

I slowly crept down the hallway and tiptoed along the edge of each stair, trying to keep them from creaking beneath my weight. I could feel the cold metal in my hand as I tightened my grip around it before turning toward the kitchen. As I rounded the corner I saw a shadow at the sink and my heart skipped a beat. I raised my hand, ready to do harm, as they turned around.

A shirtless Grant eyed me suspiciously as I lowered my arm and brought my hand to my chest, trying to catch my breath.

"What the hell are you doing in here? You scared the shit out of me!" I quietly exclaimed, trying to not wake the kids up.

"I'm getting a drink of water…" He stepped closer and narrowed his eyes as he tried to figure out what I was holding in my hand. "What exactly are you doing?"

"I was having a bad dream, and then Annie started talking in her sleep which freaked me out. Right after she said it, I saw a shadow in the hallway and I came to investigate," I explained with a shrug of my shoulders.

"So instead of coming to get me, you decided to come sneak up on a possible burglar, and use this as your weapon?" he asked as he reached out and took it from me. "What is this?" He pulled his eyebrows together as he looked back and forth between me and it.

I had to stifle a laugh when I saw him holding the cosmetics case that I had picked up at the store earlier. It had an assortment of makeup brushes and other beauty tools inside, but I had liked it because of the sleek, metal case that it came in. I pulled my mouth into a thin line to keep from laughing as I answered him with the most serious tone I could find.

"It's a cosmetic case," I said, squaring my shoulders and tilting my chin up toward him. He arched an eyebrow and turned to look at it, studying it intensely.

"Okay… so what exactly were you planning to do? Pin them down and give them a hideous makeover? Pluck their eyebrows until they begged you to stop?"

I narrowed my eyes at him as I heard the laughter he was trying to keep out of his voice.

"I'll have you know that there are sharp scissors in there… And I know how to use them." I pursed my lips as we continued to have a stare down.

He nodded his head as if he was giving me the benefit of the doubt before he turned away and slid the lock on the side, opening the case and revealing the contents. He chuckled as he pulled out the smallest pair of grooming scissors I had ever seen.

"You're right, I wouldn't want to be caught alone in a dark alley with you if you were packing these bad boys," he said as he turned to cough to hide the laughter that was getting harder to suppress.

"You are such an ass." I rolled my eyes and held out my hand. "Give me those before you hurt yourself."

He laughed and closed the case, handing it back to me as our hands briefly touched each other. I let out a heavy sigh, thankful for the comedic relief- as brief as it was. My mind had already gone back to the nightmare and the fact that I had heard Annie talking to someone while I was trying to wake up. I felt a shiver jolt through me and wrapped my arms around myself to stop it.

"What did Annie say in her sleep that you freaked you out so bad?" he asked with genuine sincerity.

"I'll see you later, grandpa." I cringed as the words slipped off my tongue and watched as his body tensed when he heard it.

"Okay, yeah, that would freak me out too. Does she know that he's been calling?"

I nodded my head no, unsure of what else to say. My mind was already playing tricks on me so it was hard to tell what was part of the dream and what was a reality, but I was almost certain that she had said it. It bothered me even more that I actually felt like someone else had been in the room. The hair on my arms had stood on end while my heart practically raced out of my chest. There weren't many times that my body had that kind of reaction except when my father was around.

"So what are you going to do now?" Grant shifted his weight and shoved his hands into his pockets. I glanced behind him to the clock on the stove. It was three o'clock in the morning and way too early to be awake on a Sunday, yet I couldn't bring myself to go back up to the room and try to sleep in there again. But at the same time, what kind of mother would I be to leave my daughter alone in a room where I felt there could be some sort of a threat? Grant studied me as I worked my jaw back and forth, sorting through the options.

"Do you want to sleep on the couch and I can sleep in the hallway outside of Annie's room?"

I pulled my head back and looked at him. There was no way that I was going to let him sleep in the hallway.

"That's not necessary, thank you. I just need a cold glass of water and then I'll go back up and try to get some sleep with Annie."

"You know as well as I do that you're not going to sleep if you go back up there. And you need some sleep. How about I go up and check on both kids -- make sure everything looks fine and check to make sure no one is up there. Then I'll come down and sleep in the living room with you. If anyone is getting in or out of this house, we would hear and see them from the living room."

I licked my lips as I considered it. He had a good point. There was no exit upstairs and very few places that anyone could hide. I wasn't convinced that anyone had been in the house but I also couldn't relax knowing that someone could get into the house. With what Annie said on top of Wyatt knowing I was here and staying with Grant, I was on high alert. I agreed to his suggestion and worked on getting the pillows and blankets ready for us while he went back upstairs to check on the kids. A few minutes later, I could hear the soft sound as his bare feet padded across the tile floor, relieved to see he had put a shirt on while he was up there.

"Do you want the couch or the chair?" I asked as I stood in between both, holding up a blanket.

"Whichever you don't want is fine with me."

"I want you to have the more comfortable option," I countered and shifted my weight as I watched him.

"Let's be honest- neither of them are that comfortable," he said with a chuckle. I smiled, knowing he was right about that.

After a few minutes it was apparent that neither of us could decide, nor were we relaxed enough to fall asleep anytime soon. At Grant's suggestion, we curled up under blankets and sat next to each other on the couch as we watched reruns on tv. The anxiety I had been feeling since I woke up from the nightmare started to ease as I felt my body gravitate toward his. The warmth of it was so welcoming and relaxing that I found myself leaning against him as he wrapped an arm around me and held me. Soon our breathing had fallen in sync, just as quickly as our heartbeats did. With every breath we took together, I could feel our bodies melting into each other as we peacefully drifted to sleep.

There were plenty of things that I had tried to control in my life. Having our children wake up to find us asleep in each other's arms wasn't one of them.

"How could you, dad?!"

Liam's voice startled us awake, the look of anger on his face evident as he stormed off and slammed the door upstairs. I saw Grant lean his head back as he closed his eyes before I scooted over so he could get up. He pulled the blanket off and tossed it next to me on the couch as he went upstairs to talk to Liam. I shook my head, disappointed that we had let this happen. This wasn't the message that either of us wanted to send to the kids. As I glanced to the side, I saw Annie sitting at the kitchen table, looking at me with tears in her eyes.

Fifteen
Grant

I took the stairs two at a time, trying to catch up to Liam as he stormed off. There was zero intention of having Lacey in my arms last night, let alone falling asleep with her still cuddled up to my chest. I let out a quick breath of air as I climbed the last step, making my way to Liam's room as the door slammed shut in my face. I gritted my teeth, reminding myself to try not to lose my temper. He was upset by what he had seen, and rightfully so. Still, we were going to have a quick conversation about his rude behavior after we finished talking about the problem at hand.

I clenched my jaw as I knocked on his door, trying to bring my blood pressure down quickly before walking into the hot zone that was waiting for me on the other side. After a few seconds of complete silence, I knocked again.

"Go away! I don't want to talk to you!" he screamed from the other side, reigniting the flame of my temper. I rolled my neck back quickly as I tried to alleviate as much tension as possible before I turned the knob and opened the door. I saw him sitting on the edge of his bed, arms folded as he glared at me with his head lowered while he pouted.

"When I knock on your door," I pointed to it now standing wide open behind me. "It's out of respect. You're getting older and I would like to be able to treat you like a man." I spoke slowly with a firm tone. I waited for him to look up and make eye contact with me before continuing. His blue eyes that matched mine looked up, tears forming in the corners.

"However, if I'm going to treat you with respect, I expect it from you in return. Slamming your door in my face and telling me to go away— that's far from being respectful. Part of being a grown-up and acting like a man is knowing how to handle situations when you're upset and angry. So we'll keep working on that, okay?" I eased up some and noticed when his shoulders started to drop some once he calmed down. Renee had always joked that he was my mini-me, in every way possible. Little did she know just how true that was. I watched as he struggled with his emotions while waiting for me to continue with the lecture.

"Are you ready to talk about what happened downstairs and why you're so upset with me?" I asked cautiously, not at all prepared to have this conversation with him. He looked away and exhaled heavily through his nose as I watched his temper start to swell again.

"Liam..."

"It's not fair!" he shouted so loud that it startled both of us. I walked into the room and sat down on the beanbag chair that was so worn out it could explode at any minute. I took a slow breath in, hoping he would see me do it and do the same.

"What's not fair?" I tilted my head slightly to the side, catching his eye as he tried to look past me.

"That you're trying to replace mom. Lacey is nice but she's not my mom and she's never going to be."

His words tore through me like a knife, cutting deeper than I ever imagined they would. I had thought about this conversation plenty of times in the past four years, but I never thought it would be a reality. That was the main reason that I had never bothered with trying to date after Renee. Not only was I unsure whether my heart could handle it, but I was also absolutely positive that Liam's couldn't.

"Son, Lacey isn't trying to be your mom. No one— I repeat— NO ONE will ever replace your mom. The love you have for her will never change. Okay?"

He nodded forcefully as his jaw stayed clenched.

"Nothing is going on between me and Lacey. She had a bad dream last night and I offered to hang out on the couch with her while we watched TV until she could go back to sleep. It's no different than what we do when you have a bad dream," I explained, his face softening a little as I said it.

"I know that it had to be hard for you to see me with someone other than your mom, and I'm sorry. I really am. But Liam, at some point, there may be another woman in my life. Another woman in OUR lives. And I hope that you will always know that she will never replace what your mom meant to either of us and that you'll give her a chance to be part of our lives."

My heart felt like it was breaking as I talked to Liam about this. Thoughts of Renee filled my head while thoughts of Lacey tried to join in. There was a clash between the two, making me increasingly uncomfortable as I tried to sort out how I felt about both. Guilt weighed heavily on me as I thought about what I was saying to Liam and I wondered if he knew I was lying about Lacey as much as I knew I was. My head wanted to say the words that I knew my son needed to hear but my heart wanted to say the words that neither of us could handle. I was starting to move on.

After a lengthy talk with Liam, I felt mentally and emotionally exhausted as I wandered back downstairs to check on Lacey and Liam jumped in the shower. As I walked into the living room I found Lacey sitting on the couch with Annie laying her head in her lap, fresh tears on her face. When Lacey looked up at me, I could see it on her face that they had a similar talk. I ran a hand down my face, feeling the rough scruff on my jawline as I turned and made my way into the kitchen to make breakfast. I started to question whether it had been the right call to have Lacey and Annie move in with us after all.

An hour and two fresh-smelling kids later, we were sitting down at the table for a late breakfast. Thankfully, the day was still early but it definitely did not start out how I had planned. Nor was I looking forward to the awkward silence that filled the room as we ate in silence. I hadn't had a chance to talk to Lacey by ourselves since everything had happened this morning but I could see it on her face that she hated how uncomfortable things were, the tension thickening as the minutes ticked by. Unable to take it anymore, I slammed my fork down on the table, startling everyone, including myself. I hadn't meant to be so dramatic about it but I had gotten so caught up in everything in my head that I didn't realize just how worked up I was.

I felt my cheeks flush with heat as everyone turned to look at me, Lacey's eyes wide with horror as if I had finally lost my shit. If she only knew. I struggled as I tried to think about what I was going to say now that I was on the spot.

"Okay, I think we all need to talk about what happened this morning so we can clear the air and make sure there are no misunderstandings," I said cautiously, watching Lacey to make sure she was okay with where I was going with this. She pulled her lips into a thin line and nodded as she glanced between the kids. I gave her a curt nod in agreement as I looked at Annie and Liam, their faces blank and expressionless as they waited for me to say something important. I cleared my throat and leaned back in my seat, unsure of how to start.

"Liam and I have already talked, and I know that Lacey, your mom, has talked with you as well. However, if we're all going to live here together, we need to talk about this as a family." I felt my throat tighten as I said the word, panic on my face as I looked to Lacey for help. She smiled warmly as her eyes softened, a look of encouragement on her face. I didn't want to send the wrong message by calling us a family, especially given everything that had already upset the kids. But I also didn't want them to think of this as anything other than that. I wanted Annie and Lacey to feel welcomed and at home with Liam and me, which meant that we were going to treat each other like family.

"I know that it surprised you guys this morning when you found Lacey and me asleep together on the couch. As we've explained to both of you, nothing happened other than we were watching tv and fell asleep. There are no intentions of me trying to be Annie's dad or Lacey trying to be Liam's mom, so please know that even though we will be a family, we are NOT trying to replace the parents that you guys lost. Okay?" I looked between both of them as they nodded their heads in agreement before picking up their forks and resuming their breakfast. I sighed a breath of relief that everything already started to feel a little better, the air a little easier to breathe.

I leaned forward, resting my arms on the table as I cut into my pancake with the fork. I popped the bite into my mouth and started chewing when Annie blindsided me with a question that I didn't see coming.

"Are you going to do it with my mom?" Her little voice was filled with innocence as she looked up at me with a giant smile stretched across her face. Her hand was lifted in the air, holding her fork in limbo as she waited for me to respond. I could feel the moment the pancake hit the back of my throat as I sucked in a breath of air, forcing it to get lodged. The syrup burned as it tried to make its way down past the piece of pancake that stayed stuck in place. I forcefully coughed a few times, trying to dislodge it as Lacey started to get up to help. I waved her off as I continued to cough, reaching for my water to take a drink.

I could see the blush on Lacey's neck as it crept up to her cheeks while she leaned over and whispered something in Annie's ear. She sat up straight and gave me an apologetic smile as she waited for confirmation that I was okay and not about to suffer a sticky death by pancake. I took another drink of water, relieved when I felt the lump move down my throat. Annie waited for me to swallow before she spoke, probably learning the hard way not to say anything while I had food in my mouth.

"I'm sorry for what I asked," she said as she shrugged. "I just thought that maybe you were going to do it with my mom since she's so pretty and all of the boys back home wanted to do it with her too."

Lacey and I exchanged a look as I arched a brow in question. She looked mortified as she ran a hand down her face.

"Annie, what exactly are you talking about? What do you mean by 'do it'?" Lacey asked, turning to look directly at Annie.

"You know, the hugs and hand-holding. All of the gross stuff that boys like to do. Then you guys can write each other secret notes about how you have the butterflies and make eyes at each other like they do in the movies," she explained as she pushed her food around on the plate with her fork. Lacey and I exchanged a look of relief as we listened and I was thankful not to have another uncomfortable conversation.

"Honey, that's called dating. When a boy and girl like each other, they start dating. Then someday, when they're ready, they might decide to get married. Like your daddy and I did, and like Liam's mommy and daddy did." Lacey smiled as she brushed a piece of hair out of Annie's face as she talked to her.

"Okay, that makes sense," Annie said before pulling her brows in together before she pinned me with a serious look. "So, why don't you want to date my mommy?"

My eyes darted up to Lacey's, desperate for help with how to answer that question but not finding any. No matter what I said, I was bound to be the bad guy with at least one person. If I lied and said that I didn't want to date Lacey then I risked hurting her and Annie's feelings. If I admitted that I might be interested in dating Lacey then I would risk breaking the promises that I gave to Liam this morning when I assured him that nothing was going on between us and that I wouldn't start dating again before I talked to him about it first.

"That's not an appropriate question to ask someone, especially an adult," Lacey scolded calmly as her posture stiffened. "Dating isn't something that Grant or I would take lightly, as we explained to you guys this morning when we had our separate talks. Dating when you have children is a lot different than regular dating and it's not a decision that we can make lightly. Not only do we have to decide if we are ready to date, but we also have to decide whether you guys are ready for us to date. There are a lot of things that have to be considered, but rest assured that neither of you have to worry about any of this because Grant and I are not dating."

I stayed quiet as I watched Lacey talk to the kids, both their attention focused on her. I hated that we had to have this conversation with the kids before we were able to talk about it ourselves. We had made it very clear to the kids that we weren't interested in dating anyone, especially not each other, so we both felt a strong pressure to stick with what we said. The problem was that I didn't know if either of us actually meant it.

We spent the rest of the day working on getting the room converted for the kids as well as getting Lacey set up in my room. By seven o'clock we had shifted gears to get the kids ready for their first day back at school tomorrow. Lacey was reluctant to believe that they would let Annie start tomorrow since she wasn't registered yet, but agreed to get her stuff ready anyways. It was after nine o'clock when we made our way to the bedroom, awkward chemistry sparking between us as we tried to figure out how to be in the same small space with each other.

I had cleared out the nightstand on the other side of the bed, thankful that I had bought all new furniture when Liam and I moved into this house so I didn't have feelings of guilt with letting Lacey use something that had belonged to Renee. She went to the bathroom to get ready for bed while I quickly changed in the walk-in closet. It had been a while since I had lived with a woman so I forgot how long they took to get ready for anything.

Fifteen minutes later, Lacey came out of the attached master bathroom with her hair loosely piled in a messy bun on her head while her face looked like something out of a sci-fi or horror movie. I pulled a pillow up to my face and hid behind it as I tried to stifle a laugh while she climbed into bed next to me. I could sense her irritation as she swatted at the pillow, pulling it down to force me to look at her.

"What's so funny?" she asked with a hint of annoyance in her voice, her face rigid as she waited to see if I was making fun of her.

"Nothing," I mumbled as I laughed harder, trying to hide behind the pillow again before she grabbed it and threw it across the room.

"It's just a face mask, don't be such a child," she scoffed as she rolled her eyes and pulled the pillow down behind her as she tried to get comfortable.

"That is a mask indeed," I joked, getting a side-eyed glare from her in return. She ignored me as she reached over and pulled open the bottom drawer of the nightstand and grabbed a pair of socks. They were low-cut with cartoon penguins on them. My eyes slowly moved from her feet up to her masked face as she slid them on, oblivious to the additional jokes that threatened to come spewing out of my mouth.

I licked my lips as I tried to find something else to focus on without any luck. After she slipped her socks on she adjusted the pant legs of her pajama bottoms and leaned against the padded headboard and closed her eyes. I took the opportunity to lean in and really get a look at the mask. It was a thin white paper looking mask with a gooey film underneath that was holding it in place. There were holes cut out for her eyes, nostrils, and mouth, but everything else was covered by this thin white paper. I tried to remember if Renee had ever been into this sort of stuff but nothing came to mind. I definitely would have remembered laughing at this if she had whipped one out and acted like it was nothing. I was still staring at the mask when I saw one of Lacey's eyes open and glare at me as she let out a heavy sigh.

"Are you still obsessed with my mask?" she asked dryly.

"I'm sorry, I still can't get over it," I laughed.

"You're so immature," she muttered as she closed her eyes again. "Not all of us have the skin of some twenty-year-old without a care in the world, some of us have to actually work to have nice skin and not look like we're pushing eighty."

"You act like you're so ancient," I said with sarcasm. "How old are you anyway? Twenty-one? Twenty-two?"

"A real gentleman never asks a woman her age," she teased as she opened her eyes and climbed out of bed. "Now if you'll excuse me, this old lady has to go deal with her mask."

I watched as she strutted to the bathroom and closed the door behind her. I laced my hands behind my head and laid down, knowing tonight was going to be a long night. A few minutes later Lacey made her way back to the bed, her face still moist from washing the goo off of her face. She climbed into bed and reached over to open the top drawer of her nightstand. I shook my head as I saw the giant jar of earplugs that she took out and opened, pulling two from the container and sitting them on her lap. She silently put the lid back on and set the container back in the drawer before closing it.

"Earplugs? Seriously?," I asked with a smug smile knowing what she was insinuating.

"What? I need my beauty rest and I'm not about to let some loud, cranky, grizzly bear keep me up all night with their snoring." She shrugged her shoulders as she pushed them into her ears and smiled before rolling over and facing the opposite way. I shook my head and turned onto my side as I tried to remember why I ever agreed to this arrangement in the first place. Despite the creepy face mask and childish socks, the bulge in my sweatpants reminded me exactly why I had come up with this crazy idea.

<u>Sixteen</u>
Lacey

I tapped my foot nervously as I sat in the cold metal chair outside of the Principal's office, waiting for her to come in. Grant leaned against the wall opposite of me, arms casually folded over his chest as I glanced at the long-sleeved t-shirt and jogger track pants he was wearing. I pulled at the hem of my dress pants, suddenly self-conscious about getting dressed up to meet with her, even after he assured me that it was a casual meeting. It was simply to get Annie registered for school, not a job interview.

Which was another thing that was weighing heavily on my mind. I needed to get busy looking for a job as soon as I was done getting Annie set up at school. While I had loved the busy life of the ER at the hospital, so much had changed these past few months that I suddenly felt dread about going back to the same hours and being away from Annie for long. It had barely been a little over a week since I had taken off from my father's house but in that time I was forced to slow down. There was nowhere to go and nothing to do which was an odd feeling for me. The problem was that I was starting to like the easy-going, laid-back environment that I felt at Grant's house and I could see that Annie was enjoying it too. Going back to the hospital would mean that we would have to say good-bye to all of that.

I forced out a steady breath as I looked to the side and watched Annie talking to Liam before the bell rang for him to go to class. The clock hanging on the brick wall across from me showed that there were only a few minutes left before classes would start. As if on cue, I heard the quick clicking on the tile floor as a beautiful woman wearing six-inch heels came walking toward us. Her long blond hair hung loosely down her back, swaying gently with each step as her hips threatened to hypnotize me. Her lips were painted a soft pink color that enhanced the fullness of them the closer she got. Baby blue eyes looked down at me and lit up as she reached a hand out for me to shake once she got to me.

"Hi! You must be Lacey!" Her hand was soft and warm, yet her grip was firm. She reminded me of the type of woman who has had to fight hard to get to where she is in her career and therefore she's used to having to make herself not only seen but heard.

"Hi, it's nice to meet you, Ms. Anderson." I smiled as we continued to shake hands. "This is my daughter, Annie." I nodded down as Annie turned to look at us after hearing her name. The bell rang, sending Liam off to his class as the principal showed us into her office. I was surprised when Grant didn't take off as well, assuming he had a class he needed to get to.

"You can call me Beth," she said as she rounded the oversized desk that took up the majority of the office and hung her purse on the coat rack behind her. I settled down into one of the plush leather chairs across from her and scooted Annie over toward me to allow Grant to take a seat. He shook his head no as he stood off in the corner and pressed his lips into a thin line. There was a glance that was exchanged between the two of them and it made me wonder if there was a history there. I wouldn't be surprised given that she was a beautiful woman who looked to be around his age. I tried to shake the thoughts from my head as I turned my attention back to her as she began asking Annie about the last school she attended.

I watched as she quickly typed, entering all of the information into the computer in front of her. A few minutes later she smiled as she reached behind her to grab the paper she had printed and handed it to Annie.

"This is the paperwork that you'll need to give to your teacher this morning when you get to class. Mr. Walker can show you to the classroom as well as give you a quick tour of the school." She looked at Grant and he nodded before she turned her attention back to me as Annie stood up and followed Grant out of the room. "Our school is fairly small so she should be able to find everything pretty easily. And we have a lot of helpful students here that can always show her around if she forgets." Her voice was calm as she reassured me.

I adjusted in my seat, unsure of what to do next. I had expected this process to be a lot lengthier and more tedious like it was when I first registered her in Montana. Granted her school in Montana was a lot bigger than this one, both of us getting lost several times just trying to find the office. I felt better that she was going to be in a smaller school and prayed that she would make friends and quickly and easily. Beth turned her attention back to the computer and I let out the breath I had been holding when I realized that we weren't finished after all.

"Okay, I have all of Annie's information in the system so we could go ahead and send her to class right away, but I still need to collect her personal information, as well as yours." She looked away from the computer for a quick second to flash me her perfectly straight, white teeth, before looking back at the computer.

I started to feel my heart race as I realized that I hadn't asked Grant about using his personal information, even though we were living together so it would be assumed that I would use it. But who did I list as an emergency contact? What if there was an emergency? Worse- what if my dad found us and came to the school to get Annie? Would they allow her to leave with him because this is such a small town? I felt my face go white as a ghost as I stared at her, wondering if it was too late to pull Annie out of class and take off running again. How was I going to be able to go to work every day and not be able to keep an eye on her?

A few minutes passed by as I answered her questions in a zombie-like fashion, giving her Grant's address which was met with raised eyebrows as she politely entered the information in without asking any questions. I decided to give her both of my cell phone numbers since I hadn't gotten around to canceling my old phone number just yet. In a way, I felt reluctant to because every time I saw a missed call- or ten- from my dad, it reassured me that he didn't know where we were based on the hateful things he said in each voicemail. Keeping the phone on was my new safety net that I hadn't known I would need. I tapped my fingers nervously against my leg, feeling the silky fabric of the trousers as it brushed against my thigh. I had purchased these to wear to Derek's funeral and forced myself to put them on today. For some reason, it had felt like we were going to have to audition to get Annie into the school and I felt like the more presentable I looked, the less they would be able to see what a hot mess I was.

Beth was still entering information in the computer when Grant came back in and leaned against the doorway.

"Hey, I was trying to show Annie where Nurse Lorna's office is but the room was locked and the lights were off. Is she not coming in today?" he asked as she slowly turned around and looked at him with a disappointed frown on her face.

"No, unfortunately, she decided to put in her notice. This morning. That's why I was so frazzled trying to get in this morning. Not only is it the first day back after winter break, but now we don't have a school nurse. So, I really pray that all of the ice that is covering the playground doesn't result in anyone needing a nurse since I still need to find one."

I felt Grant's eyes move toward me, knowing what he was going to do before he did it. I swallowed hard as I heard him start to speak.

"Well, that's actually funny because Lacey here is looking for a job," he paused and looked between me and Beth. "And she was a trauma nurse back home."

Beth's eyes went wide as she turned and smiled, a look of pure excitement on her flawless face.

"I know it is several steps down from the ER, but would you be interested?" she asked cautiously.

I took a shaky breath and glanced at Grant who was nodding for me to consider it. This would fix the problem that I had with being away from Annie, as well as allow me to work the same time she was in school. I wouldn't have to try to find a hospital or clinic to work in which would be nice as well, however I would have to look into what was needed for me to transition to a school nurse with the Colorado Board of Nursing. With Grant letting us live there without paying any bills, it wouldn't matter what the pay was since I would be able to put money aside for when we were ready to move out on our own while still having enough to contribute to groceries and other random expenses. I tried to keep my excitement to a minimum as I turned to look at Beth and nodded yes.

"Thank you, I would be very interested," I said as I felt the excitement course through me. I couldn't believe it, it felt like all of my unanswered prayers were coming true.

Grant left the room to go check in on a few students who were supposed to be getting things ready for his class, leaving us to finish my new hire paperwork. She expected that everything would be final in a few days, pending the background check and making sure my license covered me before she could officially offer me the job and allow me to start working. I was giddy as I walked out of her office and took myself on a quick tour of the school as I tried to process that this would now be my new work.

The sky was clear with a sun that promised more warmth than it actually provided. I stepped outside, feeling the sharp sting of the icy chill that bit at my skin. I ran my hands up and down my arms as I spotted Grant and made my way over to him. He smiled and waved before he jogged over to keep me from having to walk across the field.

The way his body moved so fluidly as he ran made me think of all of the other things it could probably do as well. My mind was exhausted from the lack of sleep I had last night while my body was on constant alert any time he was around. We had talked a few times about whether it was a good idea for us to share a bed after getting the kids situated in their room. In the end, we both agreed that we could be adults and understood that it was just sleep- nothing more- so we let the issue rest as we struggled to get comfortable last night.

I tried my best to keep things as friendly as possible but the truth was that I had been anxiously obsessing over sleeping next to him since we talked about it before the shopping trip. I even went the extra mile to buy as many non-sexy things as I could think of to keep me from getting any other ideas as we got ready for bed. I put on the hideous face mask that took forever before I could get it to stay in place because I kept laughing at how ridiculous it looked. Then there were the childish pajamas and socks that I had grabbed as well because honestly, who feels sexy with pink fuzzy penguin socks? Apparently, I do, as I imagined him pulling them off my feet with his teeth before he did unimaginable things to me.

I sucked in a deep breath as I forced the thoughts from my head right before he reached me. He was slightly out of breath but it was nothing compared to what I would look like if I had tried to run across the field in freezing cold temperatures that turned your breath to ice the moment it left your mouth.

"Hey, did you get the job?" he asked with a huge smile on his face that stretched perfectly across as tiny wrinkles appeared just beneath the corners of his eyes.

"I did, thank you," I said with a warm smile. "Well, technically it's pending a background check so I can't start until then, but that should come back clean." I laughed as I said it, imagining that it sounded as odd to him as it did to me when I heard it. I wanted to smack myself in the head and see if I could knock some intelligence back into my brain.

"That's awesome, congratulations. Why don't we do a celebratory dinner tonight?" he offered as he glanced over his shoulder to check on the few students that were arranging supplies in the field as the bell rang. I didn't want to keep him from work any longer than I already had.

"That sounds great." I nodded enthusiastically because I was actually feeling pretty on top of the world right now and couldn't remember when the last time was that someone had offered to have a celebratory dinner for me. Not even Derek made the effort and there had been plenty of things that we could have celebrated. The thought made me sad, threatening to damper my mood if I didn't shift my thoughts quickly.

"Okay, well, I'll be back this afternoon to pick Annie up." I smiled and turned to walk away when I felt his hand reach out and gently grab my arm.

"You do know that I work here and will be bringing Liam home as well, right?" he asked as he raised a brow.

"Yeah…" I narrowed my eyes at him, trying to figure out where he was going with this.

"I figured I could bring Annie home since Liam and I are going to the same place." He stared at me as if I was dense, not getting the obvious fact that he had just pointed out. While I understood that it would be easier, it felt nerve-wracking not to get her myself.

"Yeah, I know that you work here and will be bringing Liam home anyways. It just feels weird not to be here to pick her up from her first day of school."

I felt nervous as I watched his face change, relieved when it softened after he got where I was coming from. He nodded sympathetically and gave me a quick pat on the shoulder.

"I'll see you this afternoon. Her class will let out by this field and the parents wait over there." He pointed in the direction of a small parking lot that was gated-in before he smiled, waved, and jogged back over to where the students had begun setting things up. I gave a small wave, knowing he wouldn't see it, as I turned to walk away. My phone vibrated in my pocket against my thigh as I pulled it out to see Kayce's name on the caller ID. I smiled as I slid my finger across to answer it.

"Hey, did you miss me already?" I asked with a smile.

"Bill is gone! My dad said that he talked to him briefly at the gas station before he flew out of the parking lot and sped off toward the highway." Her voice was filled with panic, sending shivers down my spine.

"When did he talk to him?" I froze in place as I waited.

"This morning, like maybe an hour ago?"

"Which direction is he headed?" I asked as I looked around.

"He didn't say, he just said that he was going to go fix what needed fixing."

I ran a hand down my face as I stood paralyzed with fear, wondering where he was. The highway that went through Easterville only went two directions- north and south which left a 50/50 chance that he was already on his way to find me.

104

Seventeen
Grant

I looked for Annie while lightly jogging through the mass of first graders swarming out of their classrooms as the bell rang. My goal was to catch up to her before she made it to the parking lot to meet Lacey so I could ask her about the celebratory dinner that I had been planning all day. Lacey and I had text each other throughout the day, random stuff here and there, but mainly it was just Lacey second-guessing her decision to go home and relax while Annie was at school. I could tell that being away from her today was hard with everything they had been through, so I wanted to make tonight extra special for her.

A few minutes later I spotted the pink ribbon wrapped around her ponytail as she skipped alongside another little girl, their arms linked together. I smiled, thrilled that she had already made a friend, as I caught up to them.

"Hey, Annie," I said softly so I didn't startle her but loud enough that she could hear me over the sound of the other kids as they laughed and talked around us.

"Hi!" She looked up and smiled when she heard my voice. We were getting close to the parent pickup area and I knew I needed to talk fast if I wanted to talk to her before she got to Lacey. I also needed to find Liam and make sure he wasn't off playing with his friends as he usually was.

"I have a quick question for you." I stopped and quickly pulled her to the side to let the other kids pass, glancing up to make sure Lacey hadn't spotted us yet. Her head was down as she looked at something on her phone, a few quick glances every few seconds as she looked for Annie but didn't spot us.

"Sure, what's up?" she asked as she stopped and looked at me.

"What's your mom's favorite food?"

She jutted her chin forward as she tapped it with her finger, giving it some thought. Finally, her face lit up as she answered me.

"Pizza!"

Her smile was contagious and I found myself smiling back at her while wondering if she was telling the truth or if this was really *Annie's* favorite food.

"Is that your mom's favorite, or is that your favorite?" I asked playfully as her eyes danced wildly with excitement.

"It's momma's favorite AND my favorite! Except I only like pepperoni, mommy puts gross stuff on her pizza."

I chuckled as I listened, making note of what they liked.

"What does your mom like that's so gross?" I started making a mental list of the possibilities. Anchovies. Onions. Tomatoes. Who knew what Lacey would like that Annie thought was disgusting.

"Ugh, it's too gross to even say." She held a hand to her forehead as if the thought of it alone was too much and she might pass out. I also made a note to find out if she had been enrolled in the drama class because she definitely needed to be.

"Lay it on me." I spread my arms out to the side, making sure not to accidentally knock any of the other kids in the side of the head as they passed by.

"Are you sure you can handle it?" She eyed me suspiciously as she folded her arms over her chest, looking like a mini version of Lacey. I nodded and quickly looked past her to find her mom scanning the crowd of kids, fixated on finding Annie. We were running out of time and I needed her to spill it.

"Okay, you asked," she sighed. "It's pineapple and sausage."

I bit the inside of my cheek to keep from laughing as I quickly patted her back and thanked her for letting me know before I pointed in her mom's direction and sent her on her way. A few minutes later, I found Liam and we all made our way to the truck. The inside of the cab was noisy on the quick drive home as the kids excitedly talked about their first day of school. Lacey had turned sideways in her seat so she could face them as she listened and asked questions.

Once we were home, the kids eagerly ran upstairs to go work on their homework, leaving Lacey and me downstairs by ourselves. I wasn't sure if it was the excitement of having Annie at his school or their new room arrangement but I had never once seen Liam excited to do homework. After we got home and everyone was situated, it was already after 4:30. I wanted to get a headstart on dinner since I knew I wanted to get a pizza from Paul's Pizza. It was hands down the best pizza in Haven Brook and guaranteed to have a wait tonight since it was the first day back to school. Most families were trying to get back in the groove of things which meant no time to cook.

I told Lacey that I was heading out to go grab dinner without telling her where I was going or what I was getting. I wanted it to be a surprise and I prayed that Annie didn't lead me down the wrong path with a pineapple and sausage pizza. Worst case scenario— I would eat it because there wasn't much that I wouldn't eat but I didn't want to look like an ass if I got it wrong. I quickly glanced at the parking lot, finding a space, before jumping out and heading inside.

The bell chimed above me as I opened the door and walked in, waiting in a short line. Almost all of the tables were filled with people either sitting down to eat or waiting on their own to-go order. I quickly scanned the room as I made my way to the end of the line, chuckling when I spotted Noah and Chase sitting at one of the tables in the corner of the room. I walked over and clapped a hand on Chase's shoulder, startling him as they both turned around to see who was there.

"Looks like this is the place to be tonight," I joked as I gave Noah a quick pat on the shoulder before stepping to the side so a waiter could pass by to deliver a pizza to the table behind us.

"Cravings," they both said in unison before laughing and shaking their heads. I laughed along with them, remembering how I had practically lived here when Renee was pregnant with Liam.

"I think this place and SlowMo's are the go-to place for all pregnant women," I said as my eyes shifted over to a woman in line, rubbing a hand over her pregnant belly while she stood on her tiptoes to get a glance at the pizza options through the window by the register.

"That's because those are the only decent places to eat in Haven Brook," Noah snorted.

"Oh really? What about The Vine?" Chase wadded up the napkin he had been tearing apart in front of him and threw it at Noah's head, barely missing him.

I leaned my head back and laughed as the realization crossed Noah's face that he hadn't included their own brewery as an option, even though he ate there more than anyone I knew. I glanced at the line as a few more people had come in and knew that I needed to get in line soon or I would be stuck waiting forever.

"Alright, I'm going to go place my order. Try not to kill each other before the ladies get their food," I teased with a smile.

"You and Liam doing back to school pizza night?" Chase tilted his head up to look at me. I debated on what to say because I didn't want it to come off as something bigger than it was but I also knew that it was a small town and people were already talking about us living together. Now that Lacey had taken the job at the school, it felt more real that they would be there with us for a while. I sucked in a deep breath and held it, knowing it was better for them to find out from me than to hear it from someone else in the gossip mill.

"Actually, we're having a celebratory dinner tonight. Lacey accepted a job as the school nurse and she and Annie will be living with Liam and I for the foreseeable future." I felt my hands tremble as the words rushed out of my mouth in one long-winded sentence. There was a quick glance that was almost easy to miss between the two of them before they turned their attention back to me.

"Awesome, tell Lacey we said congratulations," Noah said as his attention shifted briefly to the waitress that was carrying a pizza box in our direction.

"Yeah, same here. Tell her that Mia and I are happy that she found a job so quickly. It'll be nice to have her around."

I looked between the two of them, waiting for one of them to say something about how crazy and reckless and irresponsible this all was but there was nothing. No hidden messages or tongue-in-cheek replies.

No judgmental looks on their faces. Both of them looked unphased as if I had just told them the score of the football game.

"Okay— you guys are freaking me out— you don't have anything to say about me having a woman and her daughter living with us when we've barely known them a week?" I studied their faces as I waited for it to come. The what-in-the-hell-is-wrong-with-you lecture that had to be brewing in their heads. Finally, I saw Chase's chest rise and fall as he looked at Noah, his lips pulled into a thin line as he rapped his knuckles on the table before turning to look at me.

"I'm going to be honest with you because I feel like that's what you're asking from us," he started and I clenched my jaw waiting for it.

"Grant, I'm not going to sit here and lecture you on what you do or don't do in your life. You're a grown man who has had to figure out a lot of really hard things on your own and I don't doubt your ability to figure this out as well. There's nothing that you should feel ashamed of by having Lacey and Annie stay with you. While we don't know what's happening in their personal life, we can tell that she needs help. And it's okay to do that for her." He stood up and faced me, his eyes softening as he started to speak again.

"You're my little brother, I know you very well and can read you like a book. So I'm going to answer the questions that you won't allow yourself to think about right now. Yes, it's okay. No, she wouldn't be upset. And it only matters what your heart wants for you and Liam."

I stared at him with a puzzled look on my face, completely unsure of what the fuck he was talking about. I shook my head and looked to Noah, hoping he could shed some light on the cryptic message Chase had just given me. I watched as the corners of Noah's lips pulled up into a smile as he stood up and set his cell phone down on top of the pizza box that had been delivered.

"It's okay to move on and be happy. No, Renee wouldn't be upset. And it only matters what your heart wants for you and Liam in regards to you questioning whether you could have a relationship with Lacey, and your worries about what everyone will think." Noah's voice was gentle as he said the words that ripped my heart open and forced me to take a ragged deep breath. I felt Chase's hand on my shoulder and turned my head to look at him.

"We're here if you need us," Chase offered as another waitress came over and handed him a box of pizza before swiping the number card from the table and heading to the back. "And it's okay to not know how to handle this. Sometimes the best things in life are those that scare us the most."

I thought about their words as they said goodbye and left, leaving me alone in line to order a sausage and pineapple pizza that now felt more significant than before.

Eighteen
Lacey

The first week working at Annie's school flew by before I knew it. I was thankful for how quickly the background check had been completed and that I was able to start right away. Knowing that my dad had left Easterville on Monday had me uneasy all week that he could show up in Haven Brook at any time. Grant and I had talked Monday night after the kids had gone to sleep and I filled him in on my conversations with Kayce and the update on my dad. We both agreed that we would have to remain extra aware for a little while longer since no one knew what direction he had gone.

The problem with not knowing which direction he went in was that there were so many small towns in between Easterville and Haven Brook, that he could be in any of them. Or he could have gone the opposite way and be headed to Denver. Five days sounded like a lot of time when Easterville was only five hours away, but each small town had another one, off in the distance. It was a cluster of small towns separated by tiny patches of absolutely nothing.

I waited for the bell to ring, dismissing school for the day. The kids seemed way too excited for the weekend given that they had only been back for a week. I packed up my stuff and slid my purse onto my shoulder, bumping my phone from the desk as it fell to the floor. I picked it up, bile rising in my throat as I saw that the fall had accidentally answered an incoming call that I hadn't heard. My fingers trembled as I slowly lifted the phone to my ear and listened.

There was complete silence on the other end as I let out the breath that I had been holding. I was about to pull the phone away and hang up, wondering if maybe he hadn't realized he called me— there were plenty of drunk dialing incidents in the past. As I started to pull the phone away I heard his voice, paralyzing me with fear.

"Hello, Lacey."

I closed my eyes and stayed silent as the warm tears started to slide down my face.

"Did you really think you could get far without me finding you?"

I pulled my bottom lip in between my teeth and tasted the saltiness from the tears. I tried to steady my shaky breaths as I listened to him talk.

"I'm your father—I will *ALWAYS* find you. Didn't you learn that the hard way as a little girl?" I recognized the menacing tone in his voice and knew that he hadn't been drinking. Yet. "I always won at hide and seek and I have a feeling you're not under the bed this time."

I opened my eyes as I heard movement at my door. Grant leaned against the doorframe casually before noticing the look on my face. I put a finger to my lips to ask him to stay quiet as I watched concern wash over his face. He rushed over and stood next to me. I could feel the warmth of his hand on my lower back as I kept the phone pressed to my ear.

"You don't have to talk, you know I like the thrill of the hunt. It's even better when I can feel how scared you are." He let out a heavy breath as if he was bored. "And Lacey— you should be terrified."

The words hit me hard as I heard him hang up. I looked up at Grant, unable to speak as I tried to process what just happened. My fingers were still trembling as I lowered the phone to my chest, my heart hammering against it.

"Are you okay?" he asked gently, his hand still resting on my back.

"Yeah, just a little shook up." I tried to force a smile but my body refused. There wasn't an ounce of happiness that could be found inside me right now. Grant nodded his head slowly before glancing up at the clock hanging on the wall above my desk.

"We need to go get the kids, they're going to be waiting at the parent pick up for us."

"Okay," I said breathlessly, "let's get going."

I tried to force the phone call out of my head as we walked quickly to meet Annie and Liam. The walk felt long in the bitter cold but wasn't nearly long enough to allow me the time to pull myself together. Annie looked up at me, the smile on her face vanishing almost immediately.

"Mama, what's wrong?" she asked as she ran over and wrapped her arms around my waist. My eyes darted over to Grant, pleading with him to help me figure out what to say to her. She didn't know about any of the other phone calls and now wasn't the time to tell her about them.

"There was a mouse in your mama's office," Grant said, looking down at Annie. "It scared your mom but we were able to catch it and set it free. She's just a little shook up about it."

I smiled at Grant as I let out a shaky breath before looking down at Annie. Her face turned up to look at me, a hint of a smile pulling at her lips.

"Mama, mice don't hurt you," she explained as she tried to hold her laughter in. "They're cute and cuddly, like Mr. Jelly in our class. Ms. Phillips said that not all mice are pets, but we got really lucky that Mr. Jelly wanted to be our class pet. Maybe that one wanted to be your pet?"

She looked up at me with the innocence of a child and I felt my heart skip a beat. She was so sweet and kindhearted that she would never think of hurting an innocent animal, let alone a rodent, so it never occurred to her that someone wouldn't want one as a pet. I brushed a stray strand of hair out of her face and tucked it behind her ear.

"Well, you know, they don't really let me have pets in my office because I have to take care of kiddos who don't feel well. I wouldn't have time to take care of a pet. But Grant made sure that he found the best home for the little guy, that's why we were a few minutes late." I watched as she smiled up at Grant with an approving nod. "Alright, it's freezing out here, let's get in the truck before we all turn into popsicles!"

I tickled her sides as she ran off toward the truck, Liam right beside her. I could hear Grant's footsteps as he walked next to me in silence.

"Thank you," I whispered loud enough for him to hear me as the kids opened the back doors and hopped up into the truck. He winked as he glanced at me before walking to the driver's side to get in.

"Hey dad, can I go to Nana's house early tonight?" Liam asked after we were on the road heading home. Grant looked at Liam in the rearview mirror before casting a glance at me.

"Did you already ask Nana?"

"Yeah, she said I could come over right after school and that Annie can come too."

I tried to keep from whipping my head around to look in the backseat, afraid of the look I would see on Annie's face when I said no. I didn't know anything about Liam going to his grandma's house but I wasn't comfortable with letting Annie tag along.

"That wasn't your place to ask, Liam," Grant scolded as he shot me a quick apologetic look.

"I know," he muttered from the back seat. "I'm sorry, I wasn't trying to be disrespectful but I didn't want to leave Annie out. She's kinda like my little sister now, I just thought maybe she could stay the night at Nana's with me."

I caught myself looking over my shoulder to find Liam shrugging his shoulders in defeat as he looked out the window. There was a look of excitement on Annie's face, happy to be included without me having to force someone to do it. Back home she didn't have many friends so her friendship with Liam had been really important to her because it was genuine and I hadn't intervened in any of it. I had watched them together the past few weeks and the longer we stayed there, the closer they got. My heart nearly burst several times when I had overheard him call her his sister and I cried actual tears when Grant told me that he threatened everyone at school that they better not mess with her.

I couldn't remember the last time that Annie had a sleepover somewhere or even the last time that she and I had been apart longer than a few hours while I was at work. I shifted in my seat as I wondered if maybe I needed to give her some space and let her be herself. Even with the fear that my dad could show up at any time, I knew that I couldn't hide her forever. Every day that passed brought about a greater risk of him finding us but I couldn't force her into a life of constant fear. My childhood wasn't hers to repeat.

I watched as we took a turn onto another street, heading the opposite direction of the house. I was relieved when we stopped in front of a small house a few minutes later, realizing that we weren't that far from

Grant's house after all. He put the truck in park and slowly turned off the engine as the kids unbuckled their seat belts and jumped out, running up the short lawn to the front porch before Liam knocked excitedly on the door.

"I'm sorry about that, he had good intentions but didn't bother to ask me about it first," Grant said as he wrapped his arms around the steering wheel and leaned against it, nodding at Liam as the front door opened and a woman with gray hair stood on the other side smiling.

"It's okay, I was just caught off guard by it. I know Annie will be excited about it but I don't want her to impose on your mother's time with Liam."

"Trust me, my mom loves kids and she would love to have Annie stay with them if you're okay with it."

I looked nervously from the house back to him as my hands fidgeted in my lap. I couldn't tell who this was a bigger step for: me or Annie. Could I do this? Was I really able to allow my daughter to stay the night with a complete stranger? Although I had known Liam from the time we had been living together, the only thing I knew about Grant's mom was that everyone loved and adored her. She was widowed at a young age when Grant was a junior in high school and never remarried.

My head whipped up to look at Grant as I felt his hand softly reach over and touch mine.

"Why don't we go inside and hang out for a bit, then you can decide what you feel comfortable doing?"

I nodded in agreement, thankful that he had such a sound and well thought out plan in mind. It couldn't hurt anything to go inside and get a feel for everything before I made a decision that was eating away at me. I worried that it would be the wrong one regardless of what it was.

A few minutes later I was wiping my feet on the doormat outside before walking into a cozy little house. I was surprised to find that everything was rather organized with very little clutter. The walls were painted a soft cream color with picture frames hung neatly down the hallway. The kitchen and living room were one big area, separated by a half wall that extended into the living room to create an island that was used as the dining table. There were two oversized couches that looked like they had pull out beds inside nestled in the corner pointed at the tv that was mounted above the fireplace.

I smiled as I looked around, noticing that the majority of the time here was spent in the living room and not the kitchen. The space could have easily been divided between the two and an actual table and chairs could have been set up, but instead, the area was taken up by the couches and a few end tables in between. We walked into the living room to find Nana sitting on one couch, while Liam and Annie sat on the other.

"Come on in, we'll make some room," she said as she patted the couch and Liam jumped over to sit next to her. Grant smiled at me as he led the way, sitting on the other side of Liam, leaving the other couch for me and Annie.

I sat down next to Annie and smiled as I took in the kind-looking woman across from me. Many times over the years, I had wondered what my mother would have looked like as she grew older. She was gorgeous with long, curly, brown hair, and beautiful green eyes. Whenever I closed my eyes and pictured her it was always the framed picture that I keep with me of her when she first met my dad. She looked so young and carefree, not a worry in the world. That's the way I've always tried to remember her because the images of her covered in bruises and blood still broke my heart to this day.

I pushed the thoughts out of my head and listened as Liam told Nana all about his school day. Her brown eyes lit up with excitement every time his voice got a little louder and she would quietly clap her hands together as he told her about his accomplishments for the day. She lifted a hand to tuck a piece of hair behind her ear, a faded gold wedding ring glistening in the sunbeam that filtered through the sheer curtains behind us. A knot formed in my stomach as I glanced down and touched mine, wondering if I would someday be her age, still wearing the promise of a love that had died.

"How was your day today, Annie?" she asked as she turned her body to face Annie, giving her her undivided attention. I looked at Annie and watched as her eyes lit up the same way as Liam's when she talked about school and the science experiment they did in class. She giggled as she talked about how the teacher cussed on accident when she accidentally tipped over the jar of liquid she needed but was quickly saved when another student rushed up to help her. Thankfully, according to Annie, it was just water and no one had to worry about turning into a zombie from the spilled liquid.

We stayed talking for half an hour, the kids still filled with excitement as they talked to Nana about everything they could think of. After they ran out of steam, Liam asked if they could go play in the spare room which was now the grandkid room and not just his room anymore. I laughed when he joked about how he used to be the baby until everyone started having real babies. He had the same dry humor as his dad, with a bit more sarcasm.

As the kids ran off down the hallway I started to feel anxious again about the thought of leaving Annie here. My fingers tapped nervously on my thigh as I stared off into the distance, absentmindedly, as Grant talked to his mom about his younger brother. I had only met him once but had heard plenty of stories in the two weeks that I had been there to know that he was definitely the wild child of the bunch. I was so lost in thought that I hadn't paid attention when Grant asked me a question. I heard my name again, snapping me out of my trance as I looked up and found them both looking at me.

"I'm sorry, what?" I asked softly, looking to Grant for help. He chuckled and tried to hide his smile behind his hand.

"Did you give it any more thought about having Annie stay over tonight?"

I felt the color drain from my face as my eyes darted over to his mom. The second that we made eye contact I immediately started to feel myself relax. There was something about her that felt so calming and I found myself being pulled in by it.

"Grant, why don't you go check the fridge for me and make sure I have plenty of chocolate milk for tonight?" She subtly nodded to the kitchen as he got up and left. I let out a shaky breath and folded my hands together in my lap as I looked at her.

"I know that you don't know me, dear, and honestly I would be more worried if you weren't nervous about leaving your child with me." She smiled warmly before continuing. "I won't pressure you either way, I respect your decision as a parent to do what you think is the right thing for your child. But please know that Annie will never be an imposition to us and she's welcome here anytime."

I nodded and returned her smile, still unsure of what to do.

"It's hard," I said quietly as I looked from her to the hallway that led to where Annie was.

"I know." She sighed and leaned back against the cushion, pulling a throw pillow into her lap as she rested her hands on top of it.

"Does it ever get any easier?" I asked with a small laugh, already knowing the answer.

"Nope. My oldest is 28 and the youngest is 24. They still keep me on my toes and I worry about them constantly. Even when there's nothing to actually worry about, I still worry. It's what we learn to do when we're unexpectedly forced to be a single parent. You push through and do things because you have to, but there's never any time to just stop and think things through. Sometimes I wish that I had taken a moment to just stop and be their mom." Her lips pulled into a thin line as tears started to cloud her eyes.

"What do you mean?" My voice was soft and gentle.

"I was always the caretaker, rushing around to make sure dinner was made and chores were done. There was always a list of things that I had to get to, things that needed my attention. But rarely did I ever stop and just be their mom. I didn't take the time to check in to see how school was going or to find out what happened with the girl they liked. Sure, I knew some of it, but it was only on the surface. I kept such a tight grip on everything, terrified that if I let up even a *tad*, that I would lose control and everything would be taken from me. I had already lost so much, I couldn't stand the thought of losing anything else."

I could hear as her voice broke at the end and knew that this was hard for her to talk about. I pulled in a deep breath and held it, hoping it would give me the courage I needed to say what I needed to say.

"I can understand that. I lost my husband three months ago in a car accident. He was rushing home because I was overwhelmed with trying to get Annie fed before I had to go back to work to cover a night shift. He was speeding and the rain was coming down hard. They said that he lost control and was killed on impact. Thankfully no one else was involved, but unfortunately for me, I will always remember it as it being my fault. If I wasn't the one who was freaking out about having things done a certain way then he wouldn't have had to rush. If I would have been able to just sit back and not try to control everything then my husband would still be here. My daughter would still have her father and I wouldn't have put her life in danger by living with my dad."

The words were out of my mouth before I could stop them, my hand quickly reaching to try to cover up what I had said. I watched in horror, waiting for her reaction as my stomach dropped. Her expression remained calm and neutral as she thought about what to say.

"That's a heavy burden to carry," she said sympathetically. I could feel the sting as the tears prickled at my eyes. I blinked quickly, trying to force them away. "But honey, you can't go on thinking that it was your fault. I know that's hard to do, trust me, but you need to let go of that guilt. It'll eat you alive if you let it."

I nodded as we turned to see Grant walk back into the room. It was silly to think that he hadn't heard the conversation given that the space was barely separated by a half wall, but it still felt nice to feel like I had some privacy to get to know his mom better.

"We should probably get going," he said as he glanced between us. "Do you want me to go get Annie?" He arched an eyebrow as he asked cautiously.

I looked at his mom and felt that same level of comfort that I had felt earlier and knew that Annie would be safe here. I straightened in my seat and forced the tiny bit of confidence that had started to blossom to come out.

"I think Annie will enjoy having a sleepover here tonight," I said as steady as I could. "I'll leave my cell phone number with you in case there are any problems, you can call--"

She held her hand up to stop me as she leaned forward and locked eyes with me.

"She won't be any problem at all, and I promise that I will call if she needs anything. Even if it's just because she misses you. I know it's hard to let them go, but I promise that she's in great hands."

I let out the breath I had been holding and forced my shoulders to relax.

"And for what it's worth, I'm a retired nurse and used to be an avid hunter, always bringing home more kills than my husband. So, as the kids would say, I'm not afraid to pop a cap in someone's ass if they try to mess with my family, and Annie is family. She will be safe here, I promise you that."

I held in the laugh that threatened to come out as I pictured her as a pistol-wielding grandma, popping caps into someone's ass. We said our goodbyes as I hugged Annie a little longer than normal. My nerves were shot to hell as I walked out the door, glancing over my shoulder to see the huge smile spread across her face. It may have been torture for me to leave her but I could tell that she was already in heaven.

120

Nineteen
Grant

"Beer or wine?" I asked Lacey as we drove toward the store to grab stuff for dinner. I could tell that she was still struggling with leaving Annie, as well as the added tension she was still feeling from the phone call she had this afternoon at school.

"Either is fine with me," she sighed as I pulled into a parking spot and put the truck in park. "Maybe wine so I can stick a straw in it and call it a day."

I tried not to laugh as she climbed out of the truck and closed the door, shoving her hands into the pockets of her coat as she shivered against the icy wind. I was relieved when she bought new winter clothes last weekend for her and Annie.

We walked into General Bob's and I grabbed a handheld shopping cart, knowing we weren't getting that much. I walked with Lacey over to the deli section, waiting for her to browse the options in the case while the elderly woman on the other side smiled and waited patiently for us. I watched as Lacey's eyes wandered over the variety of food, stopping and fixating on the fried chicken before moving back over to the salad bar options. I could see her struggling with whether to go for the fried food or to try to stick with a healthier option.

"What are you thinking?" I asked, nodding to the case as I pulled her attention away from the chicken.

"Um, I don't know. The salad looks good?" she said as if she questioned whether it really did. I arched an eyebrow at her and waited as I saw the hint of a blush creep up her cheeks. She rolled her eyes and sighed dramatically before turning to the woman and smiling.

"Fine," she said to me, turning to narrow her eyes at me quickly before returning her attention to the woman who was waiting. "I would like the two-piece — no, make that the three-piece, fried chicken meal please."

The woman smiled as she slid the door open and grabbed a pair of steel tongs, getting ready to grab the chicken.

"Wait! Just two pieces, sorry." Lacey reached up on her tiptoes to make sure the woman could hear her as she stopped with her hand mid-air, afraid to pull out a piece of chicken until Lacey made up her mind.

"Are you sure? Just two pieces?" she asked as the tongs remained suspended in the air.

Lacey worked her jaw back and forth as she tried to force herself to decide. It was like watching someone make the biggest decision of their life and I was worried that if I didn't step in soon, we were going to be the woman behind the counter's age by the time she decided.

"We'll take a full bucket, mixed, please," I said as I stepped forward, bringing her attention to me. She nodded and leaned forward as she started piling the chicken into a bucket. I looked at Lacey and lowered my voice some as I said, "The thighs are really thick but the breasts are better, plumper and juicier."

I watched as her cheeks flushed bright red and her hazel eyes nearly bulged out of her head. She looked at me as if she couldn't believe I had just said what I said. I let out a low laugh as I reached forward and grabbed the bucket of chicken that was being handed to me. "The fried chicken," I chuckled as it clicked in her head what I had been talking about.

We ordered a few sides before making our way back to the liquor department to grab a bottle of wine. I wasn't a big wine drinker so I left it to Lacey to pick one while I perused the dessert options. There wasn't much, most of the good stuff was usually gone by mid-morning since it was baked fresh daily. I found a box of fudge brownies that looked promising and tossed them in the cart, hoping that Lacey had a sweet tooth and liked chocolate.

After we got home I worked on opening the bottle of Riesling while she worked on getting dinner set up for us. She offered to set the table but I thought she might relax more if we had dinner in the living room.

In an effort to keep Liam from acting like a complete barbarian when company was around we had recently started eating at the kitchen table again, but most nights when it was just us, we would plop down on the couch and use the coffee table.

I poured two glasses of wine and carried them to the living room, setting them down on the table next to the boxes of food. Everything smelled delicious and was making my mouth water as I tried to remember the last time that I had eaten fried chicken from the deli at General Bob's. I had tried to be better about cooking for us, but when I didn't we were usually at my mom's house or we spent a lot of time eating at The Vine.

We sat down on the couch and looked nervously between each other, trying to decide who was going to go first.

"You first," we both said at the same time, laughing at how predictable it was.

I shook my head as I smiled and slid the box of chicken over to Lacey while I began to scoop mashed potatoes onto my plate. A few minutes later both of us had full plates and were digging in. I watched as Lacey ate her chicken, closing her eyes as she took a bite and let the flavor melt on her tongue. It reminded me of the night that I made spaghetti and I thought she was going to have an orgasm from that damn sauce. That had been a hard image to get out of my head this week, and now I was watching her tilt her head as she brought a drumstick to her mouth, slowly opening it as she closed her eyes and bit down.

This woman was like some sort of food erotica, making everything she ate look sexier than it should be. I shifted on the couch, pulling at my pants to try to allow some room for the erection that was growing underneath as I thought about how I wished my dick was that drumstick. She brought a finger to her mouth and wiped as she licked her lips. I quickly finished my bite before I could choke and grabbed my glass of wine, taking a long drink.

For the remainder of the meal, I tried to keep my attention focused on the food and not choking to death as she continued to moan little moans with each bite she took. Fuck if I wasn't suddenly jealous of the spoon that kept going into her mouth. A few minutes later she pushed her plate away and leaned back against the couch, resting her hands on her stomach.

"Oh my goodness, I am so full," she laughed and looked at her plate before turning to look at me.

"See, it's better that we got the bucket. You would've been disappointed if you would've stuck with your 2-piece meal." I nodded toward her plate with the evidence that she had eaten three pieces after all. She started to blush a little as she looked away and I instantly felt bad for embarrassing her. I hadn't meant to insinuate that she ate too much. Hell, I was impressed with how much she was able to eat given how petite she was.

"Well, you had me at juicy breasts and thick thighs," she teased as she licked her lips and I knew she was getting back at me for embarrassing her at the deli.

"That's usually what gets me into trouble." My eyes locked onto hers, challenging her to look away. She arched an eyebrow as she pulled her bottom lip in between her teeth.

"Hmm, I would say that you're the one that's trouble." Her eyes slowly traveled from my eyes down my body as they lingered on the obvious bulge in my pants. I watched as her breathing changed the longer she stared, the way her eyes suddenly became hooded. The urge to reach over and grab her, to pull her onto my lap and show her just how hard I was, was quickly extinguished when she suddenly took a deep breath and stood up. She loaded her arms with the plates and trash from the table before rushing off to the kitchen. I leaned back against the couch for a second and closed my eyes. I was playing with fire and I knew it. But everything about Lacey made me want to light a match and watch it burn if it meant that we gave in to this sexual tension that was radiating between us.

I stood up and took the last of the boxes into the kitchen, setting them on the counter next to the ones she had already brought in. Her head was down as she nervously scrubbed the plate in the sink.

"We have a dishwasher you know?" I asked, hoping to sound playful and not like the overly- aroused teenager that she had seen a few minutes ago.

"Oh yeah, I know. But it's just these two, figured might as well wash them since we don't have a full load." She glanced up at me and forced a smile before returning her attention to the plate that was probably now the cleanest that it had ever been.

I laughed as I walked over and opened the dishwasher, looking inside to find it full of dirty dishes from this morning and last night. Her head turned to the side, a smile pulling at her lips as she realized she was caught in a lie.

"I would really hate to see what you consider a full load," I teased before I realized the sexual tone that it was laced with. It felt like no matter how hard we tried, we couldn't escape the tension that kept building between us. She opened her mouth to respond before thinking twice about it and snapping it shut. I ran a hand down my face as I tried to figure out what to do next since everything that came out of my mouth was some sort of plea for her to have sex with me.

"So, um, what did you want to do tonight? It's your first night of being kid-free," I said trying to change the tone.

"Uh, don't remind me," she sighed as she turned off the water and dried her hands on the towel next to the sink. The look on my face must have come across as insulted because she immediately looked worried and rushed to correct what she had said.

"I didn't mean any disrespect by that, I know that you and Liam have your separate time from each other often and I think that's great. I just, I don't know. I guess I feel bad and guilty that I have time away from her? It's weird but it makes me feel like a bad mom for wanting some downtime to myself. She's a wonderful kid and I love spending time with her, but-"

I held my hand up to stop her as I watched her panic about what she was starting to feel.

"But it's okay to have time to yourself, just like it's okay for her to have time for herself. That doesn't make you a bad mom, Lacey. That just makes you a mom. The guilt mixed in with the inability to know what to do with yourself without a kid around is what parenting is all about. Except they don't tell you about it in any of those what to expect books."

I felt some of the tension ease as I saw her smile, a genuine smile, when she realized that she wasn't the only one who felt that way.

"So what's on your list for your alone time?" I asked, trying to get a feel for what she wanted. As much as I wanted to spend time with her, I would gladly back off and give her the time to herself if she asked.

"I don't know, I wasn't prepared for this," she laughed. "What do you do with your downtime?"

"Usually I soak in a hot bubble bath while drinking wine and reading celebrity gossip magazines. Then I slap on a hideous face mask and devour boxes of chocolate while finishing off the bottle of wine." I shrugged as if it was an everyday thing and watched as she rolled her eyes and started to laugh. She stepped closer and pointed a finger at me, poking me in the chest as she pretended to glare at me.

"You and those damn masks," she teased as she kept poking my chest. "You know it wouldn't hurt you to wear one. You have a dry patch of skin right here..."

Her voice trailed off as she lightly ran her finger across my forehead and down my nose. I sucked in a breath at the contact, the feel of her body so close to mine that I could smell the tropical scent of her new body wash. My eyes fluttered closed as she continued to softly run her finger across my skin, heightening every sense to the fullest. I opened my eyes and reached up, grabbing her hand and pulling it down as a look of fear crossed her face.

I tried to hold back but the electricity between us was too much for me to fight. I let go of her hand as I reached forward and gently grabbed her face, leaning forward as my lips lightly landed on hers. I wanted to kiss her harder, devour her, but I knew that I needed to go slow. For both of us. I hadn't been with another woman since Renee and I assumed she hadn't been with another man since her husband. I didn't even know if she wanted this.

Softly, I moved my lips against hers, feeling the soft breath that she let out before her lips responded. A quiet moan escaped her throat and shot straight to my dick, making me desperate for more. Her hands reached up as her fingers wound their way through my hair as our mouths worked quickly over each other. I felt her lips part as she welcomed my tongue to explore her sweet little mouth. Our breathing quickly became more ragged, our hands darting over each other's body in an attempt to fulfill the desires that were quickly building between us.

Then as suddenly as it started, it all ended. Lacey pulled away, covering her mouth with her hand as she paced back and forth, her eyes wide with shock. I stepped back and lowered my head, feeling ashamed for making a move before checking to see how she felt about it.

"Lacey, I'm so sorry, I didn't mean to-"

"No- don't apologize," she held her hand up to stop me. "I don't know what that was, that's not like me. But you didn't do anything wrong."

"I didn't mean to take advantage of you, I should have checked first," I spoke slowly, with caution to keep from making things any worse.

"I liked it…" She tilted her head at me in confusion, which was fitting because I was just as confused by her statement as she was.

"Okay?..."

"Why did I like it so much? What was that?" She started to pace again and I could tell that she was asking herself, not me. "I was married for ten years. TEN YEARS— and I never felt that level of heat!"

She ran her hands up the front of her body and shivered as if it was a reminder of what she had just felt.

"Ten years of love and marriage but never that kind of rush, that feeling of being wanted. Like I seriously feel like if we would have kept going, that I would be bent over the kitchen table while we go at it- that's how hot and bothered I got just from kissing you."

She let out a sharp breath as she looked from the table to me then back to the table. I tried to control myself but I couldn't keep from looking at the table too, hoping to get half of the visual she was getting every time she looked over at it and blushed.

"I loved my husband, I really did. With my whole heart. He was my first love. My only love. And now it feels like I'm betraying him and going against everything I promised him with our wedding vows because I'm feeling so insanely attracted to you right now and I want to have really dirty, really kinky, kitchen sex!"

I tried to turn my head to the side to keep from laughing. Her eyes got big again as she stared at me before reaching over and playfully swatted at my arm.

"Grant! This isn't funny, what am I supposed to do?"

There was a hint of laughter in her voice as she started to calm down, realizing how worked up she had gotten about it. I gently reached my hand out and was relieved when she took it. I sat on the edge of the table and pulled her close to me, holding her in my arms while I looked into her eyes.

"Lacey, there is nothing that I want to do more than have kinky kitchen sex with you, right here on this table. But there is no rush. It's whenever YOU are ready. Okay?" I raised my eyebrows and watched as she closed her eyes and nodded.

"What you're feeling is completely normal, and honestly, it feels weird for me too. As much as I want to fuck you sideways on this table, I can't stop feeling guilty that I'm cheating on my wife. Just because they're gone, it doesn't mean that we stopped loving them or caring about them. It's okay for us to still feel the weight of the grief that we carry, just like it's okay for us to decide when we're ready to move on. It doesn't mean that we leave them behind, we just learn a new way to move forward without the guilt."

I wiped the tears that started to roll down her cheeks and pulled her close to me before she could see the ones that were rolling down mine. Thirty minutes later and an empty bottle of wine, we decided to find something to entertain ourselves with that wouldn't end up being sexual. Watching movies while we were cuddled on the couch was out of the question.

"Monopoly?" She pulled her brows down and frowned at the game in my hand.

"What? It's a family-friendly game. Look— there's a family playing it in the picture on the back." I turned it around to show her.

"Fine," she sighed. "But don't be mad when I take all of your money and leave you bankrupt." She pursed her lips and gave me a smug smile as she sat down on the floor, clearing the empty wine bottle from the table so I could set the game down.

"Sounds like a typical woman," I muttered as I set it down and walked to the kitchen to grab the new bottle of wine we had opened. She reached out and playfully swatted at my leg when I came back, sitting down next to her after I refilled our glasses.

"I heard your snarky little comment before you left," she teased as she opened the box and started to unpack the game pieces.

"Good, I said it loud enough." I winked and ducked as she playfully tossed the lid to the game at my head.

"Oooh, Mr. Big Shot over here, running his mouth. Why don't you put your money where your mouth is?" She narrowed her eyes as she offered her challenge.

"You're on, but I don't think you're going to like the stakes, especially since I'm gonna whoop your ass."

"Why? What are they? Strip Monopoly?"

My eyes went wide as she said it, her cheeks flushing in response when she realized that wasn't what I had been thinking.

"I was going to have you do all of my chores but I think I like where you were going with this better." I leaned back on my hands and studied her as she tried to talk her way out of it.

"No, that's not what I meant— I just assumed that was what you would come up with—you know? Like it's a guy thing?" Her voice went up and got squeaky as she started to talk faster. "I wasn't the one trying to start strip Monopoly— I just assumed—"

"Lacey?"

"Yeah?"

"Stop rambling and get the money dealt so we can play strip Monopoly." I smiled and licked my lips as I watched her consider the proposal.

"Fine. But we play by my rules," she said, squaring her shoulders.

"Okay, lay them on me." I leaned forward and took a look at the game pieces on the board, looking for the car.

"If you land on my property, you take off a piece of clothing and vice versa. If one of us goes to jail, we take off two pieces of clothing. When we pass go, we can add 1 piece back on."

"Sounds fair," I said as I hopped up and ran into the kitchen to grab the brownies. I came back and plopped down on the floor next to her, smiling as I set the box between us. She looked down and her eyes came alive as she spotted the dessert.

Forty-five minutes later and we were fully invested in the most intense, competitive game of Monopoly I had ever played. We were both buying as many properties as we could every chance we had. Lacey was doing rather well, only missing her shoes, socks, and her shirt, while I had landed in jail twice already and had yet to pass go. Needless to say that I was feeling the heat as I held the dice in my hands while sitting in my boxers. I had one roll and needed to avoid landing on any of her property, as well as going to jail. If I could roll a five I would be in the clear and on my own property.

I took a deep breath and closed my eyes as I rolled, relieved when I opened them and saw a two and a three on the dice as they came to a stop. I jerked my hand in the air in celebration while Lacey ignored it and rolled the dice. I was out of money and almost out of clothes so it was pointless to tell her it was her turn. She moved the hat around the board, landing on the Community Chest. The board had been good to her so far but I was hoping that her luck would soon run out.

Her face fell as she looked at the card in her hand that was sending her straight to jail. She looked up at me as she lowered the card to the table as she worked her mouth side to side.

"Well, I'm getting tired so I guess we can go ahead and call the game. We can call you the winner if you want, given you've already lost so much," she teased as she nodded toward the pile of clothes off in the corner by the fireplace.

"Nope, I don't think so." I shook my head and leaned forward to pick up the card. I set it in front of her and smiled the cockiest smile I had. She was right where I wanted her and I wasn't about to pass on this opportunity. I sat back and rubbed my hands back and forth in excitement as I watched her pretend to glare at me.

"I believe that card says 'Go To Jail' which according to YOUR rules means that you lose 2 pieces of clothing... and you only have 3 left. So Lacey, what do I get to see first? Top or bottom?" My voice was getting a little husky from the arousal that was coursing through me as I waited to see what she was going to take off.

She pulled her shoulders back and took a deep breath, exhaling slowly. Her eyes looked up and met mine, a nervousness behind them.

"I hate you right now," she said smugly as she stood up and started to pull her pants down over her hips, letting them fall to her feet. She stood before me wearing nothing but a black lace bra with black cotton boy short panties.

"These were your rules sweetheart," I replied with a wink. "But I have to admit that strip Monopoly might be my new favorite game."

Her fingers slid down and hooked into the top of her panties, starting to lower them before she stopped. A sexy smirk started to cross her face as she reached up and slowly slid one strap of her bra down her arm. She held the top in place with one hand while she worked the strap down the other. My eyes watched hungrily as her hand reached around the back to unclasp the bra when she stopped again.

I looked up and found her eyes focused on me as she slowly slid her hands back down over her stomach, skimming over the top of her panties as she ran the palm along the thin fabric that covered her. She kept eye contact with me as she continued to run her hand over herself, slowly moving it under the top of her panties. My dick was uncomfortably tight as it throbbed in my boxer briefs, desperate for a release as I watched her fingers move inside of her under her panties.

"So, which one do you want me to take off? Bra? Or panties?" Her voice was barely above a whisper as she kept touching herself while I watched, the thin lace of her bra shifting slightly with every movement as it threatened to slip off of her.

"Both," I growled as I got up and stood next to her. I wanted to touch her, to strip her of her clothes but I needed to know that she was ready this time.

She pulled her hand out and gently pushed her panties down, letting them fall to the floor as she stepped out of them. I sucked in a breath as I watched her reach up and unclasp her bra, letting it fall to the floor next. She was completely naked and unbelievably beautiful with the perfect curves that I couldn't wait to run my hands over. I reached down and slid my boxers off, chuckling as I heard her gasp when she saw how hard I was. I reached down and grabbed it, slowly pumping my fist around it as she watched.

I had never touched myself in front of a woman before and was worried that I was going to come in seconds with how arousing it was to have her watching me the way she was. Her fingers trembled as she reached down and ran a finger in a lazy circle around the head. I closed my eyes and groaned as my head fell backward.

Her hand ran over my mine, gently pushing it away as she took over touching me. Her hand was much smaller than mine, making my dick look even bigger in her delicate hand as it jerked back and forth over my long shaft. She watched me intently as she increased her pressure, nearly sending me over the edge. I reached down and softly held her hand in place, needing her to stop before I came all over her.

"Lacey— are you sure you want to do this?" I asked breathlessly, eager for her to answer.

"Yes," she whispered before reaching up and wrapping her hands around my neck, pulling me in as she kissed me. This kiss was different than before. Instead of soft and gentle, it was urgent and needy as her lips crushed down against mine.

I wrapped my hands around her waist, letting them slowly move down over her ass, feeling the soft skin beneath my fingers as I dug my fingers into the round globes. I reached down and lifted her, feeling the warmth of her pussy as her legs wrapped around my waist. Her breasts were soft and full as she pushed herself against me, as desperate to feel me as I was to feel her.

I walked the short distance to the kitchen and stopped in front of the table. She broke away for a quick second to glance at the table before she started giggling.

"You're not serious!" she shrieked excitedly as I set her down on top of it.

"You bet your ass I am," I growled as I slowly pushed her back so she would lay on her back. My eyes slowly trailed her body as she slid back to keep from falling off, her hands sensually rubbing over her hard nipples. "Now lay back so I can see how good you taste."

Her eyes widened with shock as she propped up on her elbows.

"You already had dinner," she teased playfully.

"Yup, and now I'm having dessert." I liked my lips and waited for her to lay down so I could run my tongue inside of her and confirm that she tasted as delicious as I imagined.

"That's why you bought brownies," she said, nodding to the living room where we had left them.

"You're right. I'll be right back." I smiled and rushed off, hearing her giggle as she laid naked on the kitchen table. I bent down and grabbed the brownies then hurried back to the kitchen.

"Alright, lay back and let me enjoy my dessert," I instructed as she watched me open the box. She laid back and adjusted herself before leaning her head to the side to watch me. I pulled a fudge brownie out and set the rest on the chair beside me. I ran a finger along the top, pulling some of the fudge off before extending my finger to her. She lifted her head off the table as she pulled my finger into her mouth, sucking the fudge off with such an intensity that it made me wonder what it would feel like to have her do that to my cock.

I slowly pulled my finger out as she laid her head back down on the table. My first instinct was to ignore all of the foreplay and just fuck her, right then and there. But I wanted to take my time with her and show her how much I wanted to be with her. Something told me that she needed me to take my time with her because no one else ever had.

Focused on teasing her as much as possible, I carefully placed small pieces of the brownie along her body, starting at her breasts and ending at the sweet spot that I couldn't wait to get to. I leaned down, careful not to smash the brownie underneath me, as I licked up the first piece in between her breast while gently caressing both breasts in my hands. I could hear a soft moan as her back slightly arched off the table, urging me to continue. My tongue leisurely trailed across one nipple, pulling it into my mouth and sucking before moving over to the other.

Her fingers wrapped around my head, running through my hair as her body responded beneath me. I slowly moved along the trail of brownies, licking up each one as I worked my way down her stomach. There was one piece left and I was anxious to devour it. I looked up and watched her as I let my tongue trail over her flushed skin, licking up the last piece of brownie before dipping down and flicking it over her clit.

She gasped as she nearly shot off the table, her legs falling to the side, allowing me direct access. I spread her legs as I dropped to my knees and licked up the wetness that was waiting for me. My tongue focused on her clit, circling the overly sensitive area while I slid a finger inside of her. She bucked beneath me as she moaned, quickly rotating her pussy around my face to get the friction that she needed. I pushed my fingers in and out of her, amazed at how wet she was as I thought about how good she was going to feel with my cock buried deep inside of her.

I focused on her breathing, knowing she was getting close as I fucked her harder with two fingers and sucked her clit. Her orgasm was fast and intense as her walls tighten around my fingers with each spasm that shook through her. Once she was done, I slowly pulled my fingers out and stood up, seeing the most beautiful woman looking completely satisfied, sprawled out on my kitchen table.

"I want more," she whispered as she bit her lip and reached forward to pull me on top of her. I wasn't sure that the table was sturdy enough to hold our weight but several thrusts later it was still standing as I came inside of her.

I felt slightly embarrassed about how fast I came but she didn't seem to mind when I offered a do-over upstairs in the bedroom. While things seemed fine between us on the surface, I couldn't help but wonder if there wasn't a ticking time bomb of grief lying just beneath the surface, ready to explode at any second.

THE TIES THAT BIND

Twenty
Lacey

My body was sore in the most wonderful way when I woke up the next morning. I don't know if it was the bottles of wine that we drank or the fact that I didn't have any responsibilities for the first time in eight years, but last night I had totally let go and surprised myself with how bold I was with Grant. The initial kiss in the kitchen had thrown me off and I wasn't sure how I felt about it, but as the night went on everything felt so right between us. So easy and comfortable, almost like how things used to be between Derek and me when we first started dating.

I used to believe that the chemistry was still there for us, that if we had the chance to rekindle that spark it would surely ignite a fire. But after Annie was born it felt like that spark was almost non-existent. I finally realized last night that I had been making excuses all of these years about why Derek and I hadn't been romantic with each other and blamed it on being exhausted and too busy with work and having a child. But the truth was that we had fallen out of love and never stopped long enough to realize it.

Sure I still loved him, nothing would ever change that. But the kind of love I had for him wasn't the same as the love I could feel myself having for Grant which terrified me. With Derek, we were a team. We shared chores and responsibilities with Annie but it didn't go much deeper than that. In the few weeks that I had lived with Grant, things fell so easily into place for us with the kids. Neither of us overstepped and I didn't have to worry about asking him to watch her for a few minutes so I could run to the store or go take a shower. As weird as it was, we all sort of just fell naturally into this perfect, little, blended family that worked together to keep everything running and each of us checking in to make sure everyone was happy.

I rolled over, surprised to find that Grant was already out of bed since we didn't have the kids this morning. Maybe it was my silly girlish expectations from watching too many romcoms, but I had pictured us waking up together, cuddling as we thought about the wonderful night we shared. Then it hit me that we hadn't bothered to talk about what last night was and I had no idea what he was wanting out of this. We had both promised the kids that nothing would happen between us unless we talked to them first. Needless to say, we had already broken that promise, however, we still owed it to ourselves and each other to talk about it before they got back and things got awkward.

I got up and slid on the pair of sweatpants and T-shirt that had been tossed to the floor when we came up here last night for round two. I didn't know what time the kids were coming back so I wanted to make sure we had time to talk before then since it was already after eight. I made my way down the stairs and paused for a minute as I heard Grant on the phone. I didn't want to eavesdrop but couldn't easily make it back up the stairs without them creaking underneath me which left me stuck in place in the middle of the stairs. I was in the processing of trying to turn around so I could attempt to quietly sneak back up the stairs when I heard Grant's voice getting louder as he came around the corner out of the kitchen.

He stopped mid-step and looked at me with surprised humor on his face while he mumbled something into the phone before covering the mouth piece with his hand.

"What are you doing?" he asked quietly as he tried to keep from laughing at my awkward position. I was bent over, ass up, as I hung on to the banister beside me to keep from falling. I had quickly panicked when I heard him and my instincts— as stupid as they were— were to try to crawl up the stairs because that would be faster and less awkward.

"I didn't want to eavesdrop," I whispered loud enough for him to hear as I shrugged in explanation.

"So you're crawling up the stairs so I can't see you?" The smile quickly spread across his face as he tried to focus on his phone call. He nodded toward the living room as he walked that way and sat on the couch. I stood up and walked down the stairs as I tried to pretend like I wasn't a complete dork this morning.

"I don't see why that would be a problem, but let me ask her real quick," he moved the mouthpiece part of the phone behind his face so he could talk to me. "It's my mom, she wanted to see if the kids could stay with her for the rest of the weekend. They started a massive puzzle last night and the kids are excited to see if they can finish it by tomorrow. She said she can bring them back around dinner time on Sunday so they have time to get back into the routine for school."

It took me a few seconds to process the question as I was struggling with how much I already missed Annie but I couldn't remember the last time she had this much fun with someone her age. I shut my eyes and took a deep breath as I tried to let go of all of the insecurities that I was feeling. When I opened them I found Grant looking at me with empathy on his face.

"Yeah, that sounds fun. I'm sure Annie will have a great time," I said as my voice betrayed me and cracked, revealing the true emotion behind my words. I forced a smile as I stood up and walked into the kitchen, not bothering to listen as Grant talked to his mom.

I stood at the coffee pot with shaky hands, trying to pull myself together. It was only a few days, it wasn't like I was going to lose Annie forever. We had always been close but after Derek died I felt like there was a deeper bond between us and part of me was terrified to let go of her because I didn't want to risk losing it. Tears started to run down my face faster than I could wipe them away. I heard footsteps behind me and quickly turned my head away to keep him from seeing me cry. I felt his hand softly touch my lower back, bringing immediate comfort with it.

"Lacey?" he asked quietly.

"Yeah?" I whispered, reluctant to turn around and face him.

"Annie's on the phone and wanted to say hi. I think she's missing her mom a little bit this morning."

I turned around to look at him and found a soft smile on his face as he handed me his cell phone before leaning forward and gently kissing my forehead. I took the phone and waited until I heard him walk away before I sucked in another deep breath and tried to keep the emotion out of my voice.

"Hey, princess! How's my sweet girl this morning?" I said excitedly, wishing I could hug her and see her beautiful face.

"Hi, mommy! I'm good! We stayed up late last night building a 5000 piece puzzle mama! It's HUMONGOUS! I've never seen one this big, but Miss Sue said that we can stay with her all weekend and help her finish it."

I could hear the excitement rushing through the phone as she talked and closed my eyes as I pictured her precious face lit up with happiness. In the background, I could hear Grant's mom telling her to call her Nana instead of Miss Connie and laughed when I heard her joke about how it made her feel ancient to be called Miss in general. Annie giggled and apologized to Nana before reassuring her that she wasn't ancient. A few seconds later she was back on the line talking to me before she got distracted by Liam showing her something. I laughed as I realized how silly I was being for worrying about her when she was clearly having a wonderful time. We said goodbye and she promised to call me tonight with an update on the puzzle and her day.

I hung up the phone and went looking for Grant to give it back to him when I heard a knock at the door. I froze in place, unsure of what to do. I had no idea if he was expecting anyone but I was pretty sure he wasn't. And in the few weeks that I had been staying there, it wasn't common for people to just drop in unannounced. I glanced down the hallway and saw the bathroom door closed as someone knocked again. Whoever it was apparently came by for a reason so I tucked Grant's phone into my pocket and walked to the door, reaching up on my tiptoes to look through the peephole before opening it.

I rolled my eyes when all I could see was the back of someone's head as they turned facing the street instead of the door. I slowly turned the doorknob and opened the door, feeling relieved when the person turned around and I recognized it was Grant's youngest brother, Wyatt. I offered a smile as I pulled the door open further and stepped to the side so he could come in.

"Hi," I said, hoping it didn't sound as awkward as it felt. He smiled a crooked smile that I imagined melted women's panties as often as Grant claimed when he was telling me that his brother had taken on the new role of the town playboy after Noah settled down with Jade.

"Mornin," he replied, his voice a tad bit deeper than I had remembered from the last time I had talked to him, though it was too brief to really remember much. He stood in the entryway and shoved his hands in his jeans as he looked around for Grant.

"He should be out in just a minute," I explained as I glanced past him to the bathroom. "Do you want some coffee?" I silently prayed that he did so I would have an excuse to walk away and make myself busy doing something other than standing awkwardly with the brother of the man I slept with less than 12 hours ago.

"That'd be great, thank you."

I smiled as warmly as I could, trying to force the corners of my lips to pull up enough to keep it from looking creepy. I slipped past him and darted into the kitchen as I heard the bathroom door open. I could hear Grant's footsteps coming down the hall as I grabbed another coffee mug out of the cabinet and set it on the counter before filling three cups from the fresh pot Grant had recently made.

"Hey, what's up man?" Grant asked as he walked into the living room. I listened as his voice moved around the small room and could tell that he was by the couch now. I guessed that Wyatt was already in there and sitting down when Grant realized he was there. I topped off the last cup then set the pot back on the warmer, debating whether or not to start a new pot. I had no idea how long Wyatt would be here and whether they would want another cup. Deciding against it, I grabbed the creamer out of the fridge and fixed Grant's coffee the way he liked it.

I didn't want to look like I was trying to play hostess in a house that wasn't technically mine, even though I was living there, but at the same time, I didn't want to be rude when I had offered to get Wyatt coffee. I carried their cups of coffee into the living room and set them on the coffee table as they both smiled and looked up at me.

"Do you want cream or sugar?" I asked Wyatt, hoping to get out of their hair as quickly as possible. It felt strange being there and I couldn't imagine that whatever brought Wyatt over this early on a Saturday morning was something that he wanted to discuss with his brother while I sat in the corner and listened.

"No thank you, this is fine." He picked up the cup and slightly lifted it in the air as a thank you before taking a sip.

"Sounds good, I'll let you guys be so you can talk." I turned to walk away when Wyatt spoke.

"Actually, I'm here to talk to you." He lowered his cup and set it on the coffee table as he shifted on the couch to turn to face me.

"Me?" I asked confusedly as I pulled my brows together.

"Yeah, I ran into a guy named Bill…"

His eyes locked onto mine and I felt the color drain from my face as I stared at him in disbelief. A shiver ripped through my body leaving an icy chill behind.

"What are you talking about?" Grant asked, taking over the conversation. Wyatt turned his head and looked at him, a seriousness on his face that resembled Grant when I first met him and he saw the bruise on Annie's cheek.

"I was out of town for work this week and decided to stay the night in Eastern Point because another storm was supposed to roll through and I didn't want to risk getting stranded. There's a little bar there that the locals hang out at, it's kinda like the town gossip mill – anyways, I was having dinner when some crazed looking man approached me, asking if I had seen his missing daughter and granddaughter." Wyatt paused and turned his attention from Grant back to me. "He showed me a picture of the three of them together and expressed how concerned he was because his drug addict daughter fled town and kidnapped his granddaughter that he has full custody of after her father recently passed away."

I covered my mouth with my hand, my fingers trembling as I listened. I was comforted knowing that he wasn't in Haven Brook yet, but it was still unsettling to know that he was close. I vaguely remembered seeing the signs for the exit to Eastern Point on my way to town but in my frenzied state to get away, I had no idea where along the road I had seen them before I had the accident.

"Son of a bitch," Grant muttered under his breath and dropped his head into his hands as he leaned forward on the couch.

"So I came by to find out what the fuck is going on," he shifted his attention from me back to Grant. "And what the fuck you got yourself into."

His words stung me as he spit them out and I realized that he was right. I had absentmindedly drug Grant and Liam into this mess, not worrying about how it could impact them if my dad showed up here. My stomach dropped when I thought about the danger I had put them in, knowing there was no easy way out of it now.

"What did you say?" Grant asked him as he looked up and locked eyes with him.

"I told him that I wasn't from around there, that I was just passing through for work. He didn't ask anything else after that and I didn't tell him anything more."

"Good, that's good," Grant said as he nodded his head. His eyes wandered over to mine and I felt the anxiety start to rise inside of me as I thought about how things would have to end before they could even start.

"You're not going to run, Lacey. We've already talked about this," he said gently, keeping his eyes on me. I could feel the intensity of the look from Wyatt but kept my eyes on Grant. This was all too much to deal with.

"I have to," I whispered. "I have to go before it's too late."

"No, you don't. You can stay here and I'll protect you and Annie, just like I promised."

"I can't put you and Liam in that kind of danger. Anyone I talk to is at risk when it comes to the people he will go through to get to me. You. Liam. Your mom. Mia. Jade. The list is getting really long, really quick. I can't let him hurt anyone else. I have to go."

Wyatt sat on the couch, taking in our conversation without saying anything. I knew that once I was gone they would talk about this and I prayed that Grant would remember that I never wanted to bring any harm to any of them.

"Look, I don't need to know the details of what's happening, I just need to know one thing—are you in trouble?" Wyatt looked directly at me as he asked the question that I couldn't answer. The tears started to run down my cheeks as I closed my eyes and shook my head. This was like a living nightmare that I would never be able to wake up from.

"That's all I needed to know." Wyatt stood up and walked around the end of the coffee table to where I was standing. My eyes fluttered open when I saw his tall frame standing in front of me.

"My brother doesn't let people in easily and yet he's let you in. I know for a fact that he hasn't been with another woman since Renee, so whatever this is—it's important to him. You're important to him. And that means that you're important to me now too. I agree with Grant, you don't need to leave. You should stay here where we can all work to protect you. I know what he looks like and I can easily find out if someone new pops up in town, asking around." His tone was gentle despite his deep voice. When I looked up at him I no longer saw a man who intimidated me, I saw a man who was being genuine and sincere.

"Thank you," I whispered, unable to say anything more. He smiled and nodded before turning away to talk to Grant who had now stood up and was standing next to us.

"It's probably a good idea to let Chase and Noah know what's going on so they can keep an eye on any new people hanging out around The Vine. The more of us who know what's going on and who to look for, the easier it will be to know when he's here." Wyatt explained to Grant who nodded in agreement.

"Do you really think he's going to come this way?" I asked with hopeful desperation in my voice. Wyatt nodded his head as he worked his jaw back and forth.

"Eastern Point is only a few hours away and I overheard him say that he's made it through all of the other towns between Easterville and Eastern Point. He's stopping in each one but he hasn't changed direction so I think it's inevitable. And there aren't that many other towns between here and Eastern Point so I think it'll be sooner than later."

I felt my body go numb as the words between Wyatt and Grant floated around me, my mind unable to process what they were saying. A few minutes later, I smiled as Wyatt waved goodbye and Grant walked him to the door. I sat down on the couch and stared off into space as I thought about what all of this meant. My mind raced as I thought about the possibilities of everything that Wyatt had suggested. Would we really know that he was here before he found me first? Would he show up at The Vine and tip off Noah and Chase before he lurked around town in the shadows, trying to find me on his own? Was he still drinking while he was going from town to town looking for us, or had I pissed him off enough to sober him up enough to plan things out? The couch shifted as Grant sat down next to me and placed a hand on my thigh, pulling me from my hopeless trance.

"You okay?" he asked quietly.

"I don't know, honestly. That's a lot to take in." I let out a heavy sigh and turned to look at him.

"I know, I'm sorry that it wasn't better news."

"Yeah, finding out that my dad is going town to town, asking people about his drug-addicted daughter who kidnapped his grandchild isn't the best news to get."

The problem with being new to a small town was that you were automatically considered suspicious by the locals. Add that to another new person coming through town, spreading terrible rumors and making you out to be some sort of monster and people would turn on you in a hurry. Which meant that if he talked to anyone in town before he talked to Chase or Noah, they would immediately freak out and point him in my direction because they would fear that it was true.

"No one in town is going to believe that, Lacey," he tried to reassure me.

"No one actually knows me. They'll freak out and think they're doing the best thing by pointing him in my direction because there's a child involved and they wouldn't want to risk her being in danger," I countered.

"People here are smart, they know that if you're staying with me, that you're not a bad person. This town has known my family for so long that they know that we are good people who only hang out with good people. You're going to be fine here, I promise."

"How does Wyatt know that we had sex?" I asked without realizing I was shifting gears and changing the topic.

"What are you talking about?" he asked confused with an eyebrow arched.

"He said that he knew for a fact that you haven't been with anyone since Renee, and that I must be important if you were with me. I'm paraphrasing but that was the gist of it."

Grant sighed and rolled his head back, stretching his neck. He ran a hand down his face then turned to look at me.

"Wyatt was the one person that I was the closest to when Renee was sick and going through her treatments. She thought it would be funny to make Wyatt agree that he would try to get me laid after she was gone so I wouldn't turn into a bitter, lonely, unhappy old man. He joked and asked her how she knew that I wouldn't go find someone on my own and she said 'because I know him too well'. The day he gets laid will be the day you show up at his house and another woman answers the door with a look of pure satisfaction on her face. If she looks pissed off -- they haven't had sex yet." He chuckled as he said it and watched for my reaction as I felt the blush creep up my neck.

"Well, I guess I should have answered the door pissed off then, huh? Protect your secret a little while longer," I teased.

"Eh, I kinda like the thought that you had a look of pure satisfaction on your face instead. Besides, it wasn't going to be long before people started to assume anyways." He shrugged as if it was no big deal.

"So, how do you feel about what happened? We never got around to talking about what all of this means and what we would want or expect from it," I asked cautiously as I eased into the topic.

He let out a slow, steady deep breath as he took a minute to think before answering me.

"Honestly, I don't know. I thought that this would be some crystal clear turning point, that I would have these signs that would tell me what to do and how to feel, but I have nothing."

"Do you regret what happened?" My tone was harder as I braced myself for his response and the high likelihood of rejection.

"Do I regret making you come four times? No. Do I regret eating fudge brownie off of your naked body while I slipped my fingers inside of you? No. Do I regret how good it felt to be so deep inside of you as you rode me on the stairs last night because we couldn't wait to make it to the bed? No. I don't regret a single thing about what happened between us last night, Lacey, and I hope that you don't either."

I felt the goofiest smile spread across my face as I bumped my shoulder against his, feeling the same giddiness from last night flow through my body at the memories of all the dirty stuff we did.

"I don't regret any of it either," I admitted, looking down at the wedding ring on my finger. "I feel kind of guilty though."

"Why is that?" He leaned back against the couch and pulled me closer to him. I let the warmth of his body flow through mine as I thought about how to say it.

"Because I never felt that way with my husband and in a way, it feels like I cheated on him. I think if sex with you would have been similar to what I had with him, I wouldn't feel as guilty about it. But it was better. A LOT better, and that makes me feel really guilty."

"I get it, that makes sense."

I swallowed hard and tried to force the new tears away.

" I felt guilty too," he confessed quietly. "Guilty for still being here, enjoying life, and having mind-blowing sex with another woman when my wife wasn't given a chance to live her life. She was always so focused on being the best mother to Liam and the best wife for me that she rarely did anything for herself. I realized recently that I didn't even know what she liked before she passed. She didn't take the time to do anything for herself and I was too selfish working at a job that sucked everything out of me that I didn't do anything for her either. I took her for granted and now she's gone." His voice cracked and I could feel the tension in his body as he tried to hold it together.

I twisted around and looked up at him as I pressed my hand to his cheek. I didn't say anything because I knew there were no words to say that would ease the pain he was feeling.

"It's okay to not be okay, Grant. Even if it's just once when no one else is around. It's okay to break down and allow yourself to feel whatever you need to and let out everything you've been holding in," I said quietly as I held his face in my hand. His eyes filled with tears as he tried to look away before I pulled his chin back in my direction and held his gaze. "It's okay, I promise."

His eyes closed as the tears started to run down his face. I gently wrapped my arms around him, just enough to comfort him without making him uncomfortable. His body trembled beneath me as he sobbed harder, trying to catch his breath. I didn't bother to wipe away the tears that ran down my cheeks as I shared in his grief with him.

"I didn't tell her that I loved her enough, she didn't know how much she meant to me," he choked out between sobs. "I should have made love to her every day and cherished every minute with her but I didn't. I didn't appreciate the time we had together when we still had it and now I'm stuck with this ache so deep inside of my chest that I feel the walls caving in as I struggle to take a breath." His words were scattered between sobs but still made perfect sense because it was exactly how I had felt after Derek died.

"I know, I know," I softly whispered in his ear as I continue to hold him.

"No one ever understands—it eats you alive to have to deal with this on top of everything else, all by yourself."

"I understand," I cleared my throat and spoke a little bit louder so he could hear me. "Losing someone we love is always hard, but losing someone that we thought we would be with forever—there's no grief that compares to that. The loss of someone that we shared all of our deepest, darkest secrets with and made plans with for the future. The loss of someone that spoke so deeply to our soul that a part of us died with them, yet we are forced to try to carry on as if we are whole. There's different grief that we feel when we lose a spouse and that grief is so consuming because it carries over into every single aspect of our lives. It's hard and no one should have to experience this."

He pulled back and looked at me, tears stained on his beautiful face as he looked deep into my eyes.

"That's why you can't leave, Lacey. You have to stay and let me protect you because there is no way that I can live through losing another woman that I care so deeply about. I couldn't save Renee, but I can save you. Please, don't make me go through this pain again, Lacey, I don't think I could survive it a second time." His voice cracked as his eyes pleaded with me and in that instant, I felt the shift that rocked my world as I knew it.

Twenty One
Grant

It was dumb of me to break down with Lacey this morning and I had been kicking myself for it ever since. After four years I thought I had finally learned to deal with the pain of losing Renee and was starting to move on, then out of nowhere, this beautiful woman comes crashing into my world and changes everything as I've known it. Talking to Wyatt this morning opened my eyes to how real the threat of Lacey's father was. He wasn't just a bad man that Lacey talked about from her childhood, he was really the crazed lunatic that was going town to town, making up terrible lies to find her and Annie. My stomach knotted when I heard that he was in Eastern Point, knowing that he could be in Haven Brook by lunchtime.

There weren't many towns along the way which meant that Haven Brook was likely his next stop. I was feeling thankful and relieved that the kids were with my mom through tomorrow night so I could have a little more uninterrupted time to think about what to do when he got here. I hoped that he would stop by The Vine or SlowMo's as they were the only places to pop in and talk to the locals, but who knew what his plans would be. We assumed that he had just stopped in Eastern Point and immediately began asking around but I had to consider whether he was calculating and scoping out the town before he started asking.

Lacey had told me that he was a raging alcoholic but the information that Wyatt had given us led me to believe that he may actually be sober right now, which was even more alarming than if he was in his regular drunken state. I wanted to talk to Lacey about it but she was immediately guarded on the subject after Wyatt left and I didn't want to further upset her. Or at least I hoped that was what had upset her and that it wasn't my out of the blue confession that I had serious feelings for her after a few weeks.

I opened the fridge and looked inside, my stomach growling as I searched for something to make for us for lunch. There were very few options sitting on the shelves and I wasn't in the mood for any of them. I closed the door and walked into the living room, finding Lacey sitting on the couch, staring at the blank tv.

"Everything alright?" If she needed space to think through things I didn't want to be up her ass or hovering over her.

"Yeah, I'm just still trying to process everything and figure out what to do when my dad gets here. Part of me is still screaming for me to go grab Annie and run, get as far away as we can, as fast as we can..." Her voice trailed off as her thoughts shifted to something else that left a saddened expression on her face.

"But?"

She waited a moment before speaking, her hazel eyes looking up at me as she contemplated whether to say what she was thinking.

"But part of me is terrified of leaving and never feeling this way again."

My heart skipped a beat as I slowly sat down on the edge of the couch and waited for her to say the words that I needed to hear her say.

"Feel like what?"

She closed her eyes and pulled in a long, slow breath before letting it out and pulling in another.

"Like I could be falling in love with you. Like I already love Liam like a son. Like I feel like we could all be a happy little family and have the happily ever after that both of us have already been robbed of once."

The smile pulled across my face before I could stop it, the ache of it one of the best feelings I've had in a long time.

"I feel like we could be really happy together too, Lacey. And I know that it's only been a few weeks and this feels totally crazy—but I'm not ready to lose you. Not even if it means that you had to run and you take Annie with you. I don't want that to happen and I'm really scared that you're going to keep considering it."

"But don't you get why I have to do it?" her voice pleaded with me to understand what her heart was trying to say. I subtly shook my head no because no matter how hard I tried, I would never understand her wanting to leave us if she thought that she might be falling in love with me and wanted to have a family together.

"I love you enough to leave. I love Liam enough to disappear and shield him from having another funeral to go to. I love you both enough to spare you the void that you're going to feel when this ends too soon because I can't stop the man who's trying to kill me. And he's not going to stop, Grant. I've seen what he can do and I know what's coming."

I sighed in frustration and ran a hand down my face. I needed her to know that there wasn't a single thing that I wouldn't do for her. When I said I would protect them, I meant it. Even if I had to use my own body as a shield to keep them safe. I had already learned by now that when her mind was set, it was set. The way she clenched her jaw told me that this wasn't a conversation that was going to go anywhere because she had already made up her mind. The only thing left to do was try to buy some time and pray that I could change her mind once her mood changed.

"Okay, how about we put a pin in this conversation for now and grab something for lunch?" I said as I stood up, hoping to change the conversation as well as the energy in the room. There was a sudden burst of energy shooting through me that made me feel desperate to get out of the house.

"Sure, what do you want and I can go make it?" She stood up and stretched before reaching up and pulling her hair into a ponytail. We both took some time this morning to get ready, even though we hadn't planned to go anywhere. As cute as she looked in her yoga pants and t-shirt, I was suddenly itching to get her out of the house and do something other than obsessing about the threat that was heavy in the air between us.

"Actually, I want to get out of the house for a bit. You okay with that?" I raised an eyebrow and waited, hoping she would say yes.

"Will Annie be okay while we're gone?" she asked nervously as she chewed on her bottom lip.

"Yeah, I'll call my mom and let her know that we're going out for a bit, and if you want, I'll ask Wyatt to go hang out there for a bit, just to be sure they're covered if they need anything."

"Okay, that sounds good. Do I need to change?" She looked down at what she was wearing before looking up at me.

"Maybe go put on something a little bit warmer and I'll pack a few things into the truck before we go."

"Are you going to tell me where we're going?" She narrowed her eyes at me suspiciously.

"Nope, now go change so we can get going," I said over my shoulder as I walked into the kitchen to pack a few things to load into the truck.

Thirty minutes later we had stopped to grab a quick sandwich and were back on the road as we headed toward Lakeview. It was a small town just outside of Haven Brook with a beautiful lake that we all used to hang out at when I was growing up. Before Renee died, we used to bring Liam trout fishing but neither of us could bring ourselves to come out here after she passed. It was a sacred memory that would forever be stored in my heart. I slowly pulled the truck around the bend, avoiding the north side of the lake where I used to go with Renee.

The lake was empty, which wasn't surprising given that it was still frozen and no one bothered to come out here in the middle of January. Something had clicked inside of me earlier and I wanted to bring Lacey here to clear her head the way I used to be able to come here and think after my dad died. There's something about the quiet calmness of the lake that really lets you do some intense soul searching. And one thing that I've learned over the years is that it's hard to do any soul searching as a single parent because you rarely get a free moment to even think for yourself, let alone get lost in thought. There may not be much that I could offer Lacey to change her mind about leaving, but at least I could offer her a chance to clear her head and make peace with the decisions she needed to make.

I put the truck in park as we stared ahead at the lake covered in thick layers of ice. The sun struggled to break free from the clouds which left it feeling a bit somber. I was about to reconsider everything and turn around to leave when Lacey let out an easy sigh and scooted forward to rest her arms on the dashboard as she stared out the window.

"This is gorgeous," she whispered.

"I was hoping you would like it," I said, feeling calmer about bringing her here.

"I love it, it's so peaceful and quiet."

"I used to come here a lot after my dad died to clear my head and try to figure things out." I felt her eyes on me as she slightly turned her head and looked at me. "Everything at home was always loud and chaotic after he died, everyone was angry about something and my mom was always super stressed out. I would sneak out and drive out here, then just sit and stare at the lake for hours. It was like it was magical, forcing all of the thoughts to the surface that I couldn't bring myself to think about at home. I would leave feeling calmer than when I first got here, and head home, ready to handle the chaos. It didn't solve any of my problems, but it definitely helped me to be able to handle them better."

"Is that why you brought me here? So I can feel calm and clear my head so I can reconsider whether I should leave?"

"No," I chuckled, loving that she was quick to call me on what she thought was some bullshit. "I brought you here because you deserve to have some downtime and peace in your life. A moment to just stop and breathe. Not have to worry about anyone or anything." I looked over at her and found her smiling at me. "Plus, we have full service out here and we're only forty-five minutes from home so we can get back quickly if we need to." I pulled my phone out and held it up for her to see, just in case she didn't believe me.

"You're too much," she joked as she leaned back against the seat and laughed. "So, what is the plan now that we're here?"

"Well, the plan is that there isn't a plan. We have lunch and no kids, so the possibilities are endless," I said as I patted the brown paper bag sitting between us on the console as I wiggled my eyebrows.

"In that case, I vote for eating. I'm starving." She licked her lips as her eyes traveled down to the bag. Something about the look on her face sent my dick into overdrive as I imagined her lips on me. As she leaned forward to reach for the bag, her t-shirt shifted, allowing me the perfect glimpse at her full breasts that were sitting heavily in a black lace bra. I swallowed hard as I tried to redirect my thoughts but I couldn't. My dick was harder than flying a kite with no wind.

"Keep looking at me that way and no one is eating lunch," she warned quietly under her breath as she grabbed the bag and looked inside. She pulled one sandwich out and turned it around to find the writing on it to see which one was hers. Her fingers grazed the side of it as she ran her hand down the length of it, intentionally fucking with my head. She casually passed me the sub sandwich and reached in to grab hers. A few seconds later she had fished out the bags of chips and napkins that were at the bottom.

I carefully unwrapped the top of it, making sure to keep the rest of it covered so I wouldn't make a mess. They had the best meatball sub in town, however, it was also the messiest sub and I didn't feel like wearing half of it. I went to take a bite when I saw Lacey set hers down on the dashboard and turn in her seat. There was a look of desire on her face, mixed in with a sexy smirk as she pulled her bottom lip in between her teeth.

I held the sandwich in the air as I watched her slowly lean across the middle console as she reached down with one hand and unzipped my jeans. I could feel the blood rushing through my ears as dirty thoughts raced through my mind of what she was about to do. She glanced up at me and smiled as her fingers slowly reached inside my boxers and pulled my dick out. She giggled when she felt how hard it was as I closed my eyes and leaned my head back, enjoying the feel of her hand on my cock.

I could feel her shift beside me as she got herself situated over the console. As I slowly opened my eyes I found her watching me with hooded eyes as she stretched across the seat, her ass in the air as she slowly lowered her mouth to my throbbing dick. Her tongue gently ran along the head, making me desperate to push her head down so I could feel her mouth wrapped around me. My breathing quickened as her tongue slowly ran up one side and down the other while her fingers reached down and ran across my balls. I shifted in my seat, the sensation almost too much when she stopped and looked up at me.

"Why don't you focus on your meatballs, and I'll focus on mine," she whispered as she nodded toward the sandwich in my hand. I was so horny and worked up that I was about ready to throw the sandwich out the window and bury my dick inside of her. She gave me a pointed look as she looked at the sandwich, then back to me, before lowering her head and pulling me to the back of her throat. My breath hitched as I jolted forward, instinctively reaching out with my free hand to hold her head in place as she bobbed up and down. I was seconds away from coming when she slowed down and pulled me out, slowly running her tongue along the sides of my cock.

I took a deep breath as I brought the sandwich to my mouth and took a bite. I had never had a woman ask me to eat a fucking sandwich while she gave me head, but here I was, eating a fucking sandwich while her brown hair flowed down her back, moving like water as she gave me the best blow job in my life. I devoured the sandwich quickly, ready to be done so I could move on to Lacey. I tossed the dirty wrapper into the back seat, thankful that I had leather seats, even though at the moment I couldn't care less about what they were.

She took one hand and brushed her hair out of her face as she slowly looked up at me, my dick still filling her mouth as she sucked me in even further. We locked eyes and never broke contact as she worked her mouth over me, sucking while working my shaft with her hand. I felt the pressure building, ready to explode at any moment.

"I'm about to come," I warned in a moan as her mouth sucked me even harder. "Now, Lacey, I'm gonna come…"

She began moving her head up and down quicker than before, creating the perfect pace as I felt the moment my orgasm pulsed through me and down her throat. A few spasms later and my body was completely relaxed as I leaned my head against the headrest and tried to catch my breath. She gently kissed the head before scooting back to her side of the truck and grabbing her sandwich.

"Man, I'm really hungry now," she teased as she leaned back and unwrapped the turkey sandwich, taking a big bite as she looked coyly at me before giggling.

Fifteen minutes later and Lacey had finished her food while my body recovered from the very unexpected but wonderful surprise. We got out of the truck and walked toward the lake, feeling the bitter chill from the water once we were only a few feet away. It was beautiful year-round but I quickly realized that beautiful didn't mean it was worth freezing my balls off to be next to it. I shivered as a gust of wind whipped through us, blowing through Lacey's hair and leaving a sweet scent behind. My body started drifting in that direction, desperate to be closer to the scent that had become almost like a drug to me.

Lacey's eyes were soft as she stared out at the lake, ignoring the cold while she was lost in thought. I could see her body trembling but didn't want to interrupt whatever was going through her mind by asking if she wanted to go back to the truck. Instead, I unzipped my hoodie and pulled it off before wrapping it around her shoulders. It was cold as fuck but I would rather that she be warm and have this time to decompress than to be warm myself. She smiled warmly as she pulled it tighter around her before she looked back toward the lake. I decided to give her some space and walked back to the truck, remembering that I had packed a few things before we left including a heavier jacket. I opened the door and reached behind my seat to grab my jacket when I saw a new text message and a missed call on my cell phone that was sitting in the drink holder in front of the middle console. I glanced over at Lacey before picking it up and seeing that both were from Wyatt.

I opened the text message first and rolled my eyes when all it said was: call me. I closed the message and went to the voicemail, listening to it before calling him back. The message was quick, asking me to call him back as soon as I got it. There was something different in his voice but I couldn't figure out what it was. I looked at the time of the missed call and messages then glanced at the current time. It had only been ten minutes so not too terrible. I grabbed the jacket from the backseat and pulled it on, then pressed send to call Wyatt back. The phone didn't even get through one full ring before he answered and I realized what I had heard in his voice. Fear.

"What's up?" I asked, still watching Lacey as she leaned against a tree and gazed out to the water.

"Lacey's dad is here," he blurted out quickly in one anxious breath.

"Here, where?" I immediately started to panic, wondering if he meant that Bill was at my mom's house, which is where Wyatt was supposed to be while Lacey and I were at the lake.

"Sorry, he's in Haven Brook. Not at mom's," he explained quickly. "Didn't mean to panic you, but either way—the fucker is here and Chase said that he's already asking around about Lacey and Annie."

"Fuck," I muttered as I ran a hand along the back of my neck, squeezing it to relieve some of the mounting tension.

"I'm here at mom's and she's aware of everything that's going on. Noah offered to come by and help but Jade wasn't feeling well so I told him to stay with her."

"Does anyone know that the kids are at mom's?"

"I have no idea, it's a small town. I could take a shit and someone would know what color it was without me telling them."

I cringed at the analogy and rolled my eyes at how direct he was, though I wasn't surprised given this was who he was all the time.

"Okay, I'll tell Lacey and we'll head back to town," I said as I started walking to where she was.

"Do you think that's a good idea?" he asked, stopping me in my tracks.

"Why wouldn't it be?" I pinched the bridge of my nose in frustration that the problem was here in front of my face and I had no idea how to handle it.

"Because he's here asking about her but doesn't know that she's actually here. If you come back, there's a chance that he will see her. If you stay out of town for a little while longer and the kids stay here with mom and me, there's a chance that Chase can convince him that she's not here and he'll keep moving."

I took in a deep breath and held it for a minute before forcing it out when I realized that he was right. Wyatt might be known as the town's playboy with no desire for responsibility, but for those of us who really knew him, he was one of the most reasonable, logical, problem solvers that I had ever met. He was right and as much as I knew that Lacey would hate the idea of being away from Annie during this ordeal, there weren't any better options to choose from.

"Okay, you're right. I'll talk to Lacey and let her know what's going on. Are you staying at mom's from here on out?"

"Yeah, I told the kids we would have a slumber party tonight so they didn't think anything odd was happening. Liam seemed a little suspicious but he went along with it once he saw how excited Annie was. Where are you guys planning to stay so I know more or less where to find you?"

"We're at the lake in Lakeview, I'll check around and see if I can find us someplace to stay for the night and let you know. Keep me posted if anything happens—and I mean ANYTHING. I'll keep my phone on me and the volume turned up."

"Sounds good, stay safe," he said before hanging up.

I glanced at Lacey as I hung up the phone and made sure the ringer was on and turned up. She looked so peaceful that I didn't want to have to go give her the bad news and ruin the wonderful time we were having. While it wasn't a complete shock that he was here and in town, it still felt like a jolt to know it was really happening. Wyatt's words kept playing over and over in my ear, *stay safe,* like a bad omen.

I slid my phone into my pocket as I quietly walked over to where she was standing, trying not to interrupt. She kept her gaze on the water but her body shifted slightly to where I was now standing beside her.

"He's here," she said without any emotion in her voice. I swallowed hard, trying to force air past the lump that was forming in my throat when I heard the tone in her voice. The sound of defeat for a battle that hadn't even started.

"How did you know?" I asked quietly, staring out at the water hoping it would bring the same feeling of peace to me that it was offering her.

"Because today was too good to be true, and my friend, all good things must come to an end." She pulled in a deep breath as she turned and looked at me, fresh tears in her eyes.

"I'm so sorry," I said as I reached over and lightly wiped a tear away.

"We knew it was coming. Now we just have to figure out what to do to keep Annie safe." She squared her shoulders, ignoring the shiver that coursed through her body with the gust of wind. "So, what's the plan?"

"Wyatt is at my mom's house and he'll be there to help watch the kids. They are both aware that Bill is in town. Chase was the first to spot him and talked to him before he called to let Wyatt know since he knew we were out of town and that Wyatt would be with the kids. Everyone is alert and aware, it's just a waiting game now. I don't know if he'll stick around long and keep asking around, but Wyatt suggested that we stay out of town for now and hope that he leaves and moves on to the next town."

"I can't leave Annie there alone while he's in town. If he finds her…" Her eyes widened with panic as she stared at me in disbelief at what I was suggesting.

"I know it's scary, but I really think it's the best option. There's a good possibility that no one knows the kids are with my mom, which means he won't know where to go looking for her if he thinks she's in Haven Brook. If we go back now, we have a very strong chance of him seeing you and knowing you're there. I won't tell you what to do. If you want to go back to be with Annie, I'll figure out a way to try to sneak us back without anyone seeing you."

She looked away from me and back out to the water as she thought about it, a series of emotions flashing across her face. One final shake of her head then she turned back to me with a determined look on her face.

"I need to go back, Grant. She's my daughter and it's my job to protect her."

I hated the idea of trying to get Lacey back to town without her being seen. The last thing we needed was for one of the locals to see us driving by then run into Bill and tell him that they just saw her. If she stayed out of town it was likely that no one would remember where they had seen her last. Even if they told him that she was living with me, we wouldn't be home when he went there looking for her. There was a huge risk with what we were about to do. I nodded my head as we walked back to the truck and climbed in, the doors slamming shut and shattering the peace that we were now leaving behind us.

158

Twenty Two
Lacey

My fingers tapped nervously against my knee as I stared out the window on the drive back to Haven Brook. I had been going back and forth on whether this was the right thing to do or if I was being selfish and putting Annie in even more danger by not listening to Grant and staying away. My body felt like it was flooded with adrenaline, ready to run at any moment. Grant's hand reached over the console and gently squeezed mine, a tight smile on his face as he glanced at me before turning his attention back to the road.

"So, I have a question for you," he said, pulling my attention away from obsessing over getting back to Annie.

"Sure, what's up?" I shifted in my seat to face him, making sure his hand stayed resting on my thigh as we continued to hold hands.

"Not that I'm complaining – at all—but what was that about earlier? With the blow job?" He cast a quick glance at me before focusing on the empty stretch of highway we were on. I was relieved that he was focused on the road so he couldn't see the blush that was heating my face.

"I knew that you wanted to make today special for me and to help me relax, but I also knew how hard it was for you to go back to the lake so I wanted to take your mind off of everything. In hindsight, now I worry that it was completely disrespectful and in poor taste to give you a blow job at the lake that you used to go to with your wife and son." I let my head fall back against the headrest and closed my eyes while realizing what a huge mistake that had been. "I'm so sorry Grant, I wasn't trying to ruin the lake for you."

He let out a laugh which startled me as I opened my eyes and turned to look at him. His face was lit up with happiness as the smile pulled tight across his face, looking completely carefree.

"You don't have to worry about that but thank you," he laughed and looked out the window.

"Why not? I don't get it, what's so funny?"

"It's nothing, I'm sorry. It's just that growing up here, everyone knew that Lakeview Lake was where you went if you wanted to sneak off and have sex. It almost feels sacrilegious to go there with a girl and not get some action. Where do you think Liam was conceived?"

I burst out laughing as I covered my mouth with my hand, shaking my head as I looked at him. I playfully pulled my hand out from under his and swatted at his chest.

"Grant Walker! You took me to the sex lake?! What kind of woman do you think I am?" I pretended to be insulted as he chuckled.

"The kind of woman who lets me lick brownies from her pussy as I eat her out on the family dinner table," he joked as he winked at me. My cheeks were on fire from the heat running through them as I remembered last night and the brownie incident.

"You're a dirty, dirty man Mr. Walker," I teased playfully.

"That I am," he wiggled his eyebrows suggestively. "But you like it when I talk dirty to you so I guess that makes you my dirty, dirty girl."

"So it would seem," I laughed, noticing the sign confirming that we were now entering the town of Haven Brook as Grant took the exit that would lead back to his house. I sucked in a breath and looked around, wondering if I should try to duck down in my seat and hide to avoid having anyone see me.

"It'll be okay," Grant assured me as he took an immediate right and took a dirt road that I had never been down before.

"Where are we going?" I asked as I leaned forward and looked around, concerned that even though I was trying to avoid being seen, I would feel better if I were able to spot Bill and know his exact location.

"This road will take us the back way to my house. The locals use it on occasion but for the most part, it's usually empty. This way no one will see us driving through town and we can decrease the chance of anyone even knowing we were here."

I nodded my head and leaned back against the seat, trying to force myself to relax even though I knew it was pointless. Grant's phone started to ring, startling me with the sound as it got louder as he fished it out of his pocket.

"It's Chase," he said as he slid his finger across the screen to answer it, pushing the speakerphone button before setting it in the cup console between us. "Hey, what's up?"

"Just wanted to let you know that Bill just left The Vine. I tried to keep him here as long as I could but he was getting antsy when it started to die down and there was no one else for him to talk to. Just wanted to give you a heads up, I don't know where he's going from here."

"Thanks for the update," Grant said, looking at me to see if there was anything I wanted to say.

"Was he drinking?" I asked loud enough for Chase to hear me.

"Only water," he confirmed before covering the phone to yell to someone else to clear the table in the back.

I could feel my anxiety start to build when I knew that he was actually sober and probably had been from the minute he started looking for me. I was used to dealing with drunk Bill but I had never had to deal with sober, pissed off Bill.

"Let us know if you hear anything. We just got back into town now, I'm on the back road heading to my house." Grant said, filling the silence while I was unable to speak.

"I thought you guys were going to stay out of town for a day or two until he left?" Chase asked confused.

I bit the inside of my cheek, hearing the concern in Chase's voice about why we hadn't stayed away like everyone had discussed. Apparently, I was the only one who had thought it would be a good idea to come back, and now I was seriously questioning that decision.

"Lacey didn't want to be away from Annie," Grant explained softly. "I get it, I wouldn't be able to stay away if I thought Rylee was in trouble. We do what we have to do as parents to keep our kids safe and there's nothing wrong with that." Chase replied, making me feel better that not everyone was judging me for coming back.

"Are the kids going to stay with mom tonight or are you picking them up?" Chase asked as Grant turned down another side road and houses started to pass by my window. Most of them looked familiar and I was pretty sure we were only a few blocks away.

"I'm not sure, we haven't talked about it yet," Grant said, turning his attention toward me. "What do you want to do?"

I tried to weigh the options but it all came back around to me needing to know that Annie was safe and I couldn't trust that she was unless I could see her.

"I want to pick Annie up and take her home so I can keep an eye on her and make sure she's safe."

"Okay, I'll call my mom real quick and let her know the change of plans," Grant confirmed as he slowly turned the corner and waited before pulling onto his street. I knew that he was being cautious, making sure that no one was around watching us but it still sent a chill up my spine.

"Sounds good, Noah and I are both free if you guys need anything. Just call."

I smiled as we hung up the call with Chase and pulled up to the garage. Grant put the truck in park but didn't turn it off as he thought about what to do.

"Do you want to go with me to my mom's to get the kids or do you want to wait here to make sure everything is okay? We can go inside and check the house, then if everything is fine, I can run and pick up the kids and bring them back while you wait here for us."

His idea made a lot of sense and seemed like the most practical option that we had. Instead of both of us going to his mom's and coming back with the kids to a house that may or may not be safe, it seemed better to split up and confirm the house was safe before we brought them back. A few minutes later we made our way through the house, feeling somewhat silly as we worked as a team to clear each room, looking in closets and under beds as if there was a real-life boogeyman just waiting to jump out and scare us.

I said bye to him and planted a quick kiss on his lips before he darted out the door and hopped in his truck to go to his mom's. Even though I had planned to spend some time this weekend talking about us and what this new relationship meant to both of us, that never happened and I didn't want to get in the habit of kissing him in front of the kids before we could talk about it. I tried to make a mental note to talk to him about it tonight so we could make sure we were all on the same page before we slipped in front of the kids.

Fifteen minutes had passed while I was upstairs unpacking the things I had taken with me earlier for the lake. I heard the front door open and close, smiling when I knew that I was going to see Annie's beautiful face in just a few minutes. I waited anxiously to hear the sound of her footsteps as she came bouncing up the stairs looking for me, or the sound of her sweet voice as she called for me. I stopped for a second and listened, wondering if I had imagined hearing the front door close as it was eerily quiet downstairs for having Grant and two rambunctious kids come back.

The silence was deafening as the pounding in my ears got louder from my blood pressure rising quickly. Something was wrong, I just knew it. Annie was never this quiet, what if something happened to her? I tossed the hoodie I had been wearing that Grant wrapped around me earlier on the bed and softly crept downstairs. I glanced around in each room looking for a sign that someone was there, not seeing anything. My heart was racing as I opened the closet door in the hallway, waiting for someone to jump out and get me.

A few minutes later I rolled my eyes for having imagined hearing the door when clearly no one was there. I checked my phone to see a text message from Grant that they were packing up the kid's stuff and would be back in a few minutes. I pushed my phone back down into my pocket and made my way back upstairs, forcing myself to finish unpacking instead of worrying about checking each of the rooms again. I had checked things thoroughly while I was downstairs so the likelihood that anyone could have quietly snuck up the stairs while I wasn't looking was slim. I was being overly paranoid and needed to calm down before Annie got back and started to worry.

I quickly hung up the hoodie and my sweater from today, closing the closet door behind me. As I turned around, my heart stopped beating as I clutched a hand to my chest.

"Hello, Lacey," he growled, standing in the doorway, blocking my only way out. My eyes frantically searched the room, looking for anything that could be used as a weapon as he stepped closer. A few seconds later I heard the front door open and the sound of happy children rushing in, filling the silence between us.

"Mama, where are you?" Annie called excitedly as I heard her footsteps already running up the stairs.

Bill quickly stepped to the side, the baseball bat that I had used to knock him out before gripped tightly in his right hand. I watched in terror as I heard Annie coming up the stairs, no idea of what was about to happen as Bill hid inside the room waiting for her.

"Annie, go back downstairs, I'll be right there," I called to her quickly, as loud as I could hoping that Grant would hear the fear in my voice and know that something was wrong.

My stomach dropped as I saw her run toward the bedroom, pure happiness on her face to see me. I must have looked like I had seen a ghost because she immediately stopped and fear filled her eyes but it was too late. I watched in horror as Bill reached out to the side and grabbed her, pulling her into him as he locked one arm around her neck, holding her small body against his so she couldn't move. Her beloved stuffed puppy fell to the floor by her feet before Bill kicked it out of the way. My heart filled with sadness as her eyes watched it tumble across the room, the only thing that had brought her real comfort in the past few months was now out of reach.

"Let her go," I warned, moving closer. He raised the bat and smirked as he swung it, barely missing Annie's head by a fraction of an inch. I gasped as she closed her eyes and started to cry. Where was Grant?? I was too afraid to take my eyes off of him to try to search for something to use as a weapon.

"She's just a child," I pleaded as I watched on helplessly. Annie looked up and her eyes met mine. There was a look in them that I had never seen before as she gave me a subtle nod before lifting her foot and smashing it down as hard as she could on his. He quickly released his hold on her as he pulled his foot away, letting out a slew of curse words in the process. Annie spun around and jabbed her elbow into his nose before bringing her knee up and kicking him in the balls. Everything happened so fast that I could barely believe my eyes as I watched him crumple over in pain.

"Come on, mom, we have to go!" she screamed at me before reaching down and grabbing her puppy. Her small hand grabbed mine as she pulled me away and we ran down the hallway to the stairs. I let go of Annie's hand and smiled when she turned to look at me.

"Run fast and go find Grant," I commanded as we both started to rush down the stairs. She was almost to the bottom when I felt strong arms grab me from behind and tackle me, pulling me back up the stairs. My eyes went wide with fear when I felt Bill's arm wrapped tightly against my waist as he drug me up to my feet. Annie stopped at the bottom and spun around to look for me when she saw what was happening. Bill reached into his pocket and pulled out a lighter and a piece of cloth that reeked of gasoline. His eyes danced wildly as he let me go and pushed me to the side so I couldn't get past him as he lit the cloth on fire and watched it fall over the rail to the ground in the living room.

Within seconds a fire had started in the carpet, spreading quickly as Annie looked back and forth between the fire and me, terrified. I pushed as hard as I could to try to get past Bill, unable to move him out of the way as I watched the fire growing quickly. Within seconds I saw Grant and Liam come running in as the back door in the kitchen slammed shut. Grant's face was etched in fear as he saw the fire before looking up to find me pinned to the wall with Bill's hands wrapped tightly around my throat.

"Since you like to start fires and all, I thought you would enjoy this one. We can watch your fake little family burn together," he sneered in my ear as he held me in place. I turned my head the best I could and made eye contact with Grant. Unable to speak, I mouthed the words I needed him to hear.

Take care of my baby.

Twenty Three
Grant

I quickly dashed over and grabbed Annie, picking her up by her waist as she clutched her stuffed animal to her chest and screamed for Lacey. Within seconds I had both kids outside as the fire continued to spread throughout the living room.

"Run to Nana's house and tell her to call for help. Go!" I screamed at Liam as his eyes fearfully watched the house go up in flames. "Take Annie and run to Nana's!"

He snapped out of his daze and nodded as he reached down and grabbed her hand, pulling her with him as they took off running for my mom's house. I hated sending them off on their own but it was the safest thing I could do right now. I needed to get them away from the house while I went back in to save Lacey. I quickly looked over my shoulder to make sure they were still running the direction they needed to before I turned and ran into the house.

As soon as I ran through the door I was immediately engulfed in heat from the fire that was now crawling up the curtains and dancing across the ceiling. It wouldn't take long for the fire to go through the ceiling and spread to the rooms upstairs where Lacey was. I pulled my jacket up and brought it over my nose and mouth, trying to shield it from the smoke as I ran and took the stairs two at a time. It was already starting to get smokey upstairs, making it hard to see more than a few feet in front of me.

I heard a loud crash coming from the bedroom and took off in that direction. There were loud grunts as Lacey and Bill struggled though

I couldn't see where they were through all of the smoke. I tried to move quickly, pushing my way through until I could figure out where they were. A few seconds later I heard a loud thud followed by a body dropping to the floor. My heart was racing as I tried to find Lacey and get her out of there.

The heat was quickly spreading through the bedroom as I saw the smoke thickening and further clouding my view. I knew better than to try to call for her and risk inhaling the smoke but I was starting to feel helpless and desperate.

"Lacey!!" I screamed, hoping she would hear me and point me in the right direction to find her.

I kept walking, my hand in front of me as I tried to figure out what was in front of me, praying that I would reach her soon. There was very little time left if we were going to get out before the fire trapped us. I could hear the sound of footsteps pounding on the floor near me and turned to see Wyatt as he crouched down beside me. We looked at each other before he nodded and went the opposite way while I crawled across the floor trying to find her. As I got lower, I was able to see a little better and felt my heart skip a beat when I looked straight ahead and saw Lacey's hand covered in blood as it laid lifelessly on the floor in front of the bed.

I raced over to her, letting go of my jacket as I was forced to take in a deep breath to catch my breath. Her face was bloody and swollen, her body unresponsive.

"She's over here!" I yelled, praying that Wyatt could hear me. I had no idea where Bill was but I didn't give a fuck at that moment. My only concern was Lacey and getting her out of there. Within a few minutes, Wyatt was by my side.

"We need to get her out of here, quickly," I said as I stood up and tried to pick her up. I felt the tightness in my lungs as I took a breath, the lack of oxygen more noticeable as the smoke filled the room. Wyatt went to the other end and picked up her feet as I lifted under her arms and we carefully carried her back down the stairs. The fire was already spreading, climbing up each baluster as it reached the top of the handrail. We walked quickly, making sure we were careful not to drop her, while also making sure we got out of the way before the fire decided to take over the stairs.

A few more steps and we were down the stairs and almost to the doorway when I glanced up and saw a tall shadowy figure at the top of the stairs. I nodded to Wyatt who quickly looked behind him and turned back around. We needed to move faster. In the distance, I could hear the sirens as help was on the way. As we walked the last few steps to the door I watched as Bill made his way down the stairs, grabbing onto the wall as he coughed and struggled to breathe.

The front door was still open which made it easier for us to rush Lacey outside and lay her down in the snow-covered grass. She was still unconscious and I feared that I might have been too late after all. I reached under her jaw and felt her neck, trying to find a pulse but couldn't. My mind was racing as I tried to remember everything that I knew about CPR and prayed that I would remember what I needed to do. I bent down and listened to see if I could hear her breathing. Nothing. I was starting to panic when I saw Bill coming out of the doorway, heading straight for us.

There was no way that I was going to let Lacey die this way so I bent down and blew two breaths into her mouth before finding the spot to start compressions. He would have to kill me and pry my dead body off of hers before I would let him hurt her again. Wyatt watched on as I continued to do CPR, oblivious to the fact that danger was quickly upon us. I tried to focus on Lacey as I felt the weight of every step Bill took as he stalked toward us. My eyes stayed focused on him as he got closer, redirecting Wyatt's attention as he turned around and sprung to his feet.

I lowered my head to do two more breaths as I heard the scuffle as Wyatt started to wrestle Bill away from us. There was a loud thud as the two rolled around on the ground, Wyatt swinging as hard as he could to keep Bill off of him. I glanced up and watched as everything happened in slow motion in front of me.

Bill had rolled out from underneath Wyatt and was now hovering over him as Wyatt clutched his side and tried to breathe through the pain of the last blow to his ribs. Bill's hand reached behind his back and pulled out a knife, bringing it around and stabbing it straight into Wyatt's chest. I gasped as I watched the blood quickly turn the snow red beneath my baby brother's body. The sirens were closer but I couldn't focus on any of that right now. I had to quickly decide who's life I was going to save- my brother's or the woman I loved.

Twenty Four
Grant

"I hate this fucking hospital," I muttered as Chase sat on one side of me and Noah sat on the other. The emergency room waiting area had quickly started to fill up as my family came in for an update on Wyatt and Lacey. I glanced off to the side where my mom sat in the corner with Liam and Annie, trying to keep them calm and distracted from what was happening. I didn't want the kids to be there and I would have done anything to keep them from being there but after I was brought in for smoke inhalation monitoring, there weren't many options since my mom was stressed with having two out of three of her children in the hospital.

"I know, brother, I know," Chase said as he wrapped an arm around my shoulders and gave me a quick hug. My feet tapped anxiously on the floor as I waited for an update.

My mind kept replaying everything that happened, even after it felt like I had told the same story a hundred times already. Between giving statements to the police, the doctors, and my family, it felt like the story was on repeat but the problem was that I didn't know how it ended which kept me anxious. After the adrenaline wore off some, I was able to process everything that happened after the stabbing and the CPR I tried to do on Lacey. From what the police told me, they were already there when it had happened and they had seen everything. Apparently, in a state of shock, I blocked out the rest.

From what I was told, the police and paramedics were there immediately as they took over working on Lacey and got Wyatt into the ambulance and rushed him to the hospital. I don't remember any of it, other than hearing a loud sound, which I was told was a gunshot. After Bill refused to drop the knife and charged at a police officer, they shot him. It was a non-lethal shot and he was currently in surgery. No one had told me anything about Lacey or her condition since we got here which was starting to piss me off. They would only give updates to immediate family, which she didn't have aside from her minor child who didn't need to hear the details of what happened, and a father who was in surgery and tried to murder her.

I stood up and started pacing the hallway, hoping that someone would tell us something soon. Off in the distance, I heard Annie talking and turned around to see her on a cell phone. I pulled my brows together in confusion as I looked at my mom who shrugged her shoulders. I walked over and squatted down in front of Annie, smiling as she smiled back at me.

"Whose phone is that, sweetheart?" I asked gently, not wanting her to feel like she was in trouble.

"It's mommy's," she said happily as I heard a female voice on the other line.

"Where did you get her phone?"

"I borrowed it," she said sadly and tucked her chin to her chest in embarrassment. "I wanted to have a phone to call mommy while I was at school in case I needed her. I didn't tell her that I took her new phone."

"It's okay sweetie, I'm sure she wouldn't mind," I reassured her. "Who are you talking to?"

"It's mommy's cousin, Kayce." She smiled and handed me the phone.

"Thank you," I whispered as I took the phone and stood up, needing to give my legs a break from being in a crouching position for so long. "Hi, I know that you don't know me, but—"

"You're Grant, the single father with the heart of gold and temper of an ox," a feminine voice said on the other line.

"I am. And you must be the wild cousin, Kayce," I joked as we both chuckled.

"How is she?" she asked, a worried tone to her voice.

"I don't know, they won't give me any details because I'm not family." I ran a hand down my face and turned back to the receptionist station, hoping someone would soon be coming over to give us an update.

"What happened? Annie said that Bill was there and that she was calling me because she was going to need to come live with me when her mommy went to heaven to be with her daddy."

I heard the crack in her voice as I struggled to keep the tears in my eyes from overflowing. I looked down at Annie and wondered how she could be so strong and brave when she knew that her world might be changing forever. Was she so used to the grief of losing a parent that it didn't bother her the way it would most people? Or was she simply in shock like the rest of us and refusing to believe it?

I quickly explained everything to Kayce and gave her a minute as I heard her crying on the other line.

"I'm so sorry that I wasn't there to protect her," she whispered.

"I keep saying the same thing. Even though I was there, I didn't get to her before he could and I feel like it's my fault that she's in this hospital, fighting for her life."

"I'm going to pack up a few things and then I'll drive down there. This is my cell phone number, will you keep me updated as you know anything?"

"Absolutely," I said as I spotted a doctor come out of the double doors from the emergency room and started walking our way. I quickly wrapped up the phone call and made sure she had my cell phone number so she could call as soon as she got to town. I held my breath and waited as the doctor glanced down at the clipboard in his hand before looking up at the waiting room full of anxious people.

"Family of Wyatt Walker?" he called out.

I reached down and offered my mom a hand to help her stand up, not sure that she was going to be able to hold herself up if there was bad news. We walked a few steps toward him as Chase came over from the other side. He nodded and offered a tight smile before he started talking.

"Wyatt suffered substantial damage from the knife wound, however after several procedures, we were able to stop the bleeding. The angle that the knife entered his chest barely missed the heart which is probably the only thing that saved his life. At this point we're waiting

for him to come out of recovery, then we can further assess him.
A nurse will be out later to let you know when he can start having
visitors after he's been moved to a room in the ICU."

We all breathed a sigh of relief and thanked the doctor for the update
as he made his way back to the emergency room. I was thankful that
Wyatt was going to be okay, even if he had a long road ahead of him.
We were a strong family and we could help him through this. I sat
down and ran my hands down my jeans as my palms started to sweat
again, wishing there was something on Lacey.

I looked outside and saw the sun starting to set, casting an orange glow
across the wall which reminded me of the flames that spread quickly
up the walls of my house. It hadn't even occurred to me until now that
in addition to everything else, Liam and I now had nowhere to live. I
didn't even know if the house was still standing, but needless to say,
it wasn't safe to go into any time soon. I had been so caught up in
everything else that I hadn't had a chance to talk to Liam and see how
he was doing with everything.

Chase and Noah took off to go grab food for everyone and bring it
back which left me alone with my mom and the kids after everyone
else finally went home after we had an update on Wyatt. It was calm
and quiet in the empty room, the sound deafening as I thought about
how to talk to both kids about what had happened today. They were
off in the corner, sitting on the floor while they played a game of Uno.
Mia had been kind enough earlier to swing by with a handful of things
to keep the kids entertained after she had been unsuccessful in getting
them to go back to her house so she could watch them for us.

I walked over and sat down between them, smiling as I watched them
play. I loved the relationship that they had with each other, a special
sibling type of love that I had with my brothers. A few minutes later,
their game was over and they laughed when Annie won, again.

"Do you want to play, dad?" Liam asked as he collected the cards in a
pile and shuffled them.

"No thanks, bud. But I do want to talk to you guys about what
happened today," I said carefully, glancing up at my mom who was
pretending to read the book in her hand that had been on the same
page for ten minutes now.

"Okay," they both said, neither of them showing any sort of emotion
about it. Liam set the cards down between them as they both turned to

look at me and waited for me to start talking.

"I know that today was very scary with the fire and everything that happened with Bill," I started, looking between both of them. "Do you guys have any questions or want to talk about anything that happened today?"

They both stared at me in silence before looking at each other as some secret passed between them.

"I have a question," Liam said, turning to face me. I nodded for him to ask and waited.

"I know that I didn't want you and Lacey to date when I first thought you guys might like each other, but that was only because I didn't want to get attached and lose another person like I lost mom. I know that she isn't my mom, but I didn't want to get close to her and then lose her. But now that she might not make it," he glanced nervously at Annie before looking back at me, "I don't want Annie to have to move away with her mom's cousin. Can Annie live with us and we can protect her since her mom and dad will both be in heaven?" His eyes filled with tears as they pleaded with me.

"It doesn't really work that way, son," I said as I tried to swallow past the lump in my throat.

"But Dad, I promised her that I would protect her. If her mom goes to heaven, who will protect her if I'm not there? She shouldn't have to keep losing everyone she loves, that's not fair!" he shouted as the tears started rolling down his face. "I don't want Lacey to die, that's not fair either!" He stood up and balled his fist.

I grabbed him and pulled him to my chest as I wrapped my arms around him while his body trembled as he cried.

"I know it's not fair, but we have to stay positive and keep praying that the doctors will make Lacey better, okay?"

"Why does it even matter? They couldn't fix mom, they're not going to fix her either. I'll never know what it's like to have a mom in my life because God doesn't want to give me one. I try to be a good kid but maybe I'm not doing something right and it makes him mad so he keeps taking the people I love from me." His words shattered my heart into a million pieces as the warm tears slid down my face. I hugged him even tighter, not having the words to say what he needed to hear. My mom set her book down on the chair beside her and folded her hands in her lap.

"Come here, Liam, Nana wants to talk to you for a minute," she said as she smiled and patted the empty chair on the other side of her. I eased up on the tight hold that I had around him as he stepped to the side and sat down, looking straight ahead instead of at my mom.

"Life has been extremely hard for you my sweet boy, and I'm so sorry that you've had to go through so many challenges in the short time you've been on this earth. But that doesn't mean that you've done anything wrong. Sometimes we are dealt really bad hands in life but it's up to us to decide what to do with them. We all experience loss and some of us experience more than others. That doesn't mean that we've done anything wrong or that we deserve bad things. That means that everyone that comes into our lives plays a role and teaches us something. For example, your mom was taken from us way too soon, however, she taught you how to love with all of your heart and I will always be thankful for that. Your dad has taught you how to be strong and to do what's right. And Annie, she's taught you how to be brave."

She smiled as she looked over at Annie who smiled back at her.

"We have to take each experience in life- the good and the bad- and decide what to do with it. It's easy to play the victim and complain about the things that we don't like but that also means that we take for granted the special things that come our way as well. We don't know what's going to happen with Lacey but either way, I can see that she's made a very special impression on you and that you have sincere feelings about her. It's okay to allow yourself to love her like a mother because I can see that she loves you like a son. And both of you know that no one would ever replace your mom. She will always hold a very special place in your heart that no one can replace."

"Thanks, Nana, sometimes I forget how smart you are," Liam said, getting a full smile from my mom in return. She wrapped an arm around his shoulders and pulled him close to her, kissing the top of his head.

"So does this mean that I will live with you if my mommy goes to heaven with my daddy? Or will I have to move away again? I don't like moving," Annie said as her voice trailed off.

"Let's not worry about that right now, okay sweet girl?" I said as I reached over and pulled her over to me, giving her the biggest hug that I could without hurting her.

"Where are we going to live now that the fire burned down our house?" Liam asked as he looked between me and my mother.

"You guys will all come stay with me again until we get everything figured out. Besides, we still have that massive puzzle to finish building," my mom said with a smile as she looked between both kids before looking up at me. I was thankful for everything she had ever done for me growing up but now that I was an adult and having to deal with things on my own, I was even more grateful for her.

A nurse came through the double doors with a solemn look on her face as she walked in our direction. My heart stopped as I held my breath and waited.

"Family of Lacey Holbrook?" she asked as she looked from me to Annie, her eyes saddening when she saw her.

"That's my mommy!" Annie exclaimed as she jumped up and ran over. I climbed to my feet and took the few steps toward her, putting my hand protectively on Annie's shoulder to stop her.

"We're not family but I'm all she has besides her daughter," I looked down at Annie. "She's living with me and we're dating," I explained, regretting that this was how the kids were going to find out about us officially dating.

"I think it would be best if you came with me so we can talk in private," she said, forcing her lips into a thin line when the smile refused to go any further. I nodded and quietly asked Annie to go sit with my mom as I sucked in a deep breath and followed the nurse through the double doors. In all of the times that I had been to this hospital, the only time I had been taken to a private area for an update was when I received the news about Renee. I followed her down the long, empty hallway, stopping briefly as she opened a door and waited for me to go inside. I took a few steps in and turned to face her.

"I'm so sorry," she started as my world shattered around me, drowning out her voice as she continued to talk.

Twenty Five
Lacey

Everything around me was white and peaceful as I walked—no floated—around, trying to figure out where to go. It wasn't like there were any signs or a check-in desk that had an angelic receptionist waiting to greet me. I tried to take a deep breath, surprised by my inability to do so. Everything felt odd, different. There was no pain or anxiety, but there was also no other feeling or emotion at the moment either.

I kept floating about, drifting along the perfect white clouds, looking around as I wondered if this was my new eternity. I had to admit that it was nice and all, but I could imagine that I would get bored with this real fast.

"Hello??" I called out, my voice sounding sweeter than usual.

There was no answer so I kept floating until I came to an area where the colors started to change. The white was thinning out and suddenly I was floating through somewhere that looked very familiar. It was a happy place, I could feel it in my bones as I waited for my memories to catch up to me. A few minutes later more details started to appear and suddenly I was back at home, in Montana. Derek was in his office, while Annie and I were in the living room playing before dinner. I remembered this night, it was one of the best nights we had shared as a family.

I smiled as I watched Annie and I sneak into his office carrying a tray of cookies and a glass of milk. He had been overly stressed with work and we wanted to do something nice for him. I watched as his face lit up, completely surprised by the gesture as he spun his chair around and picked Annie up, wrapping her in a big hug. He looked up at me, a sad smile on his face that I didn't remember being there before, then reached to the side to close his laptop.

I had remembered this night so clearly, everything playing over and over again in my head on how we had been so happy and so in love, then everything was taken so quickly from us. But as I watched it now, I noticed that the happiness I remembered before wasn't really there. I was happy and Annie was happy, but Derek wasn't. I stared at him, trying to figure out the emotion that was heavy on his face that he tried to hide behind the forced smile and then recognized it from the way my mom looked growing up. Desperation.

I shook my head, unable to process what I was seeing as I continued to float by. The scene changed again and this time I felt dread as I saw the night sky covered in rain, the darkness of the night more ominous than ever. I watched as Derek left his office, glancing down at his cell phone and closing his eyes in frustration. He had been working late and just received a text from me, asking him to come home to take care of Annie so I could go in to work. We were struggling with our finances but I had no idea he was this stressed out.

I watched as he got into the car and sat down, texting me back before putting his phone into the cup holder. He started the engine and slowly reversed as he turned on the windshield wipers to clear the rain that was coming down harder. I could feel myself panicking as I watched him shift the car to drive, never putting his seatbelt on like he always did. He drove out of the parking lot and onto the main street before getting on the highway. Derek was always a cautious driver so it shocked me when I saw the speedometer quickly moving as he pressed his foot to the gas, the car going 90 mph as the rain splattered against the windshield quicker than he could clear it.

There were no other cars around as he pressed harder on the gas, forcing the car to 100 mph. Then out of nowhere, he started talking and everything went silent as I heard his final words.

"Lacey, I'm so sorry to do this to you. I don't have any other choice. I'm drowning here, literally and figuratively, so I need to set you free. Take care of our Annie and make sure she always knows how much I love my little puppy." Tears rolled down his face as he jerked the steering wheel to the right, forcing the car to spiral out of control as it hydroplaned and flew over the side of the embankment. My hand flew to my chest as I watched in horror, seeing how my husband's life had ended.

Suddenly, I felt a presence beside me and looked up to find Derek next to me, decked out in white, floating as he looked down at the scene of the accident with me. I stared at him as I tried to find the words to say to him.

"That was one hell of an accident, but I hope you know that I didn't suffer. I mean, I was suffering a lot before it happened, but I didn't suffer when it happened. It was instant," he explained, looking over at me.

"Why the hell did you do that?" I demanded, completely shocked that he was even there and I was talking to him. Okay, maybe it was more that I was shocked that I was the one who was there and talking to him.

"We were going under fast, I couldn't get us caught up on bills. We were about to lose the house, my business was going under. There wasn't anything I could do to save us. So I took the only way out and knew that you would be okay without me, that there would be enough in the life insurance policy to take care of you and Annie."

"Why didn't you talk to me first? We could have figured this out another way, Derek," I said still completely pissed at him. "And what insurance policy?"

"That was the only way, trust me. And you have to look deeper, you'll find it if you look hard enough." He started to fade away, leaving me frustrated as I begged for him to come back and finish talking to me.

I looked back down at the accident and shook my head, needing to get away from it. I floated along, praying that the next stop would be more peaceful than the last. It didn't feel like I was actually in heaven yet but I definitely wasn't alive and talking to my dead husband while being shown the truth about what happened. It seemed to be some sort of weird parallel universe that I was starting to feel desperate to get out of.

As I kept floating, I suddenly smelled the heavenly scent of fresh-baked apple pie and smiled, remembering the days when my mom would bake one with me after school. We had an apple tree out front and she always loved to collect the apples before the birds could get them, then we'd go inside and bake a pie. She would make two and let me sneak a few bites out of the secret one before my dad got home, then we would serve the other one after dinner. I loved our secret pie and enjoyed the afternoons when we would sit outside and read books on a blanket under the tree while eating it before dinner.

I floated faster, glancing around the kitchen from my childhood, relieved when I saw my mom bent over, reaching into the oven to pull out a pie. She turned around and I gasped, her face as beautiful as I remembered, frozen in time. As a child, I remembered her face bright with happiness but now that I really got a look at her and had experienced my own traumas, I saw the pain beneath the smile. Her eyes were tired and her body looked frail and weak as she turned to grab the plates from the cabinet and a row of bruises showed beneath her shirt as it lifted.

"You better get in here before the pie gets cold," she said over her shoulder before turning to smile at me.

"Hey mama, it's me, Lacey," I said as I floated in and stood on the other side of the table.

"I know who you are, sweetheart." She smiled and set the plates on the table that was now between us.

"You can see me? Like I can see you? And we can hear each other?" I asked, completely confused by what was going on. This was all a crazy, surreal dream. It had to be.

"Of course I can, silly girl. I've been watching you for years, I just didn't think I would get a chance to talk to you so soon," she said worriedly.

"I didn't think I would get to talk to you this soon either," I admitted as I shrugged. "Does this mean that I'm dead?"

She looked me over and gave me a quick shake of the head.

"Nope, not dead. Not yet."

"Well, then how am I here and talking to you?"

"Our imagination is a very powerful thing, I've always told you that," she said as she grabbed a knife and started to cut into the pie.

"You're telling me," I sighed. "So what do I do now? Just keep wandering around, talking to dead people?"

"I suppose that's up to you, you're the only one who can know what your heart truly wants."

"It's not that easy."

"Why not?" she asked, setting the knife on the table next to the pie.

"Because, I'm stuck here, in this world, or whatever it is."

"So what do you want?" She tilted her head to the side and smiled as if she already knew what I was going to say.

"I want Annie. And Grant. And Liam. I want to live and not be in fear of dad. I want to get past the guilt I feel over Derek's death. I want to be happy and live a life you would have been proud of."

"Then what are you waiting for?" she asked as she reached over and shoved me in my chest.

"What the hell was that for?!"

"Clear!" She shoved me again, harder. I watched as she started to change before me. The last thing I saw before everything went bright white was her hand reaching out and shoving me one last time, harder this time as she yelled *clear* and I fell backward.

184

<u>Twenty Six</u>
Grant- 2 Weeks Later

"What kind of Valentine's Day cards do you want to get, Annie?" my mom asked as she shuffled around the kitchen, getting breakfast ready for the kids. I glanced behind me as I reached into the fridge and saw the sad look on her face when she considered the question.

"I don't think I want to do Valentine's Day cards this year," she said quietly as she sat down.

"Why not?" I asked gently as I grabbed the gallon of milk and closed the fridge. Her sweet eyes looked up at me with the same sadness I had seen for the past two weeks since Lacey was taken to the hospital.

"Because it's a day of love and I don't feel like being lovey when I'm still so sad."

"I get it," I sighed and my shoulders fell. "And it's okay to be sad, sweetheart."

Liam wrapped an arm around her shoulders and walked her over to the couch where they sat down and watched cartoons while we finished making breakfast.

"Poor thing," my mom whispered only loud enough for me to hear. "This has to be so hard for her. First her dad, now her mom."

I nodded my head in agreement, unable to say anything about what had happened. These past few weeks had been difficult and trying with everything going on all at once. From losing the house to Lacey and Wyatt being in the hospital, it was all too much and my recent focus had been on getting the kids and I settled in at my mom's house while the insurance company worked the claim on mine. There were so many questions about what we would do next— would we knock down the rest of the house that was barely standing and rebuild? Would we walk away and find somewhere new to live? And the question that ate at me daily was whether Annie would keep living with us or move five hours away to live with Lacey's cousin Kayce.

"I heard that Wyatt might be over later today, he's slowly trying to get around on his own again," my mom said, continuing on in a one-sided conversation which she was pretty used to these days since I had become the worst company to have around.

"I'm happy to hear that he's doing better, seems his recovery is moving along at the right pace," I offered, trying to force myself to engage.

My cell phone started to ring, startling both of us the way it did anytime it rang lately. It seemed we were always waiting for a call with bad news to come. The other shoe to drop. I glanced down and saw the phone number for the hospital displayed on the screen and blew out a breath. I caught my mom's eye, a worried look on her face as we nodded at each other and I stepped outside to take the phone call.

"Hello?" I answered, trying to brace myself. I hadn't heard anything in over a week so I was on pins and needles that this was the call I had been dreading would come.

"Grant Walker?" a woman asked.

"Yes, that's me."

"My name is Marie and I'm calling from Haven Brook hospital, we have an update for you on Lacey Holbrook."

I sucked in a deep breath, allowing the cold air to burn through my lungs.

"Yes?"

"She's awake."

Twenty Seven
Lacey

I listened as the doctor talked, glancing over his shoulder every few minutes to check to see if Grant or Annie were coming. I was so anxious to see them and wrap my arms around Annie in the biggest hug ever, never letting her go. The doctor explained the multiple operations I had undergone as well as the blood transfusion I needed after everything was said and done. I nodded along, trying to take in everything while my mind wandered to more important things. Like my family.

"Do you have any questions for me?" he asked as he set my chart down on the counter behind him and folded his hands in his lap, pulling the crisp, white coat tight across his shoulders.

"Honestly, I have no idea. That's a lot to take in and for a minute there, I thought I died. I had this crazy dream where I was walking around in this white cloudy area and I got to see and talk to my dead husband and mother," I laughed, brushing it off as being as ridiculous as it sounded. His face looked grim as he pulled his lips into a thin line. "What is it?" I asked, concerned.

"There were a few times that we did lose you, and after the last one, we weren't sure that we were going to get you back. You gave us quite a scare."

I tried to process what he was saying but it seemed so unreal. I had heard of people having similar near-death experiences but I never would have believed they were real had I not had one myself. Part of me still believed that it was just a dream that was playing tricks on my mind, but the other part needed to believe it was real so I could finally have the answers that I was looking for. I wasn't ready to give up so easily on the idea that easy that my dead husband had offered me some insight into his final days just yet.

"Well, if you don't have any questions for me, then I'll be on my way. Your nurse can page me if anything comes up." He stood up and grabbed my chart from the counter.

"Do you know when I will be able to go home?" I asked.

"Given everything that you've been through, I would like to monitor you for another 24-48 hours, just to make sure you're in the clear. After that, we can talk about discharging you if you're ready."

"Sounds good, thank you," I said as he started to walk out the door. "Sorry," I squealed as I held my hand up for him to stop. "Will someone let my family know they can come back to see me now? I'm sure they're tired of sitting in the waiting room." I smiled warmly as I thought about seeing Annie.

"I'm sorry, there isn't anyone in the waiting room," he said gently as he walked back into the room and stood next to my bed. My face fell with disappointment as I looked up at him and tilted my head to the side. Why would they leave?

"No one?" I asked as my brows pulled together in confusion. He shook his head no.

"Why? Did someone force them to leave?" None of this made any sense. Grant and I were doing well before everything happened, wouldn't he be worried about me enough to stay? And did he take my daughter away from me as well? Then I realized that I had no idea what happened to Bill and whether Annie and Grant were even okay. Panic flooded through me as I tried to remember everything that happened and couldn't. How did I get out of the house? Did Annie make it out? Did everyone die in the fire except me? The monitor next to my bed started to beep loudly causing concern to flash across his face as he stepped closer.

"Everything is alright but I need you to try to calm down for me, okay?" He sat back down where he had been a few minutes ago and scooted his chair closer to me.

"Lacey, do you remember anything about what happened and why you're in the hospital?" he asked as he studied my face.

"I remember my father attacking me. He had me pinned to the wall by my throat and then I started to lose consciousness but not before he threw me to the floor and punched me repeatedly." I turned my head away and lowered my voice, embarrassed to be saying the words out loud.

"What happened after that?"

"I don't know, everything started to get foggy. I couldn't breathe, there was a lot of smoke in the room. Then I guess I passed out."

He nodded quickly and rubbed his lips back and forth together.

"Did my family die in the fire?" I asked, the words mixing with the bile that was rising in my throat.

"There was one casualty, yes." His eyes softened and he waited for me to take another breath as the alarms on the monitor started beeping again. I looked at him with tears in my eyes, begging him to tell me without making me ask.

"Your father did not survive his injuries. I'm so sorry. There were complications from the gunshot wound as well as respiratory distress from the smoke inhalation. We did everything we could but we weren't able to save him."

I covered my mouth with my hand as a loud sob escaped and my body started to tremble. *Gunshot wound?!?*

"But the rest…?"

"They're fine," he assured me with a smile.

"Then why aren't they here? I want to see my daughter, please," I begged.

"They stayed here for a while, actually longer than I've ever seen a family stick around. But after the first week, we asked them to go home and try to get the kids back to some level of normal."

"First week?" I pulled my head back in shock and frowned.

"Lacey, do you remember me telling you that you've been here for two weeks and that you've been in a coma until now?" He tilted his head to the side and waited to see if anything clicked as I remembered him telling me. I felt my cheeks blush as I got embarrassed that I didn't remember because I hadn't been paying attention. I was too distracted with thoughts of Annie.

"I'm so sorry, I wasn't paying very good attention earlier. My mind was preoccupied with seeing my daughter."

"I completely understand, I'll make sure the nurse calls Mr. Walker and asks that he bring her to see you. Try to rest and take it easy, your body has been through a lot in two weeks."

He smiled and walked out the door leaving me feeling overwhelmed with the massive amount of information he had just given me. There were still a thousand other details that I needed to know about what happened but right now, I was only focused on one thing. Seeing Annie.

Twenty Eight
Grant

"Come on guys, let's go!" I called through the house as I stood at the front door, ready to leave and get to the hospital to see Lacey. I didn't know anything other than that she was awake. After two weeks of agonizing over everything that happened and beating myself up on all of the things I should have done differently, she was finally awake.

I was an intense combination of excited and anxious, feeling like I might jump out of my skin at any moment. I had already called Kayce and given her the update as the kids worked on getting ready to go. Annie wanted to take the special cards she had been making for Lacey with us and Liam offered to help her get them together. It was adorable and so heart-warming but also slightly irritating that we were taking even longer to get out of the house and to the hospital. I had waited for this moment for what felt like forever and I didn't want to wait any longer.

I had no idea what we were supposed to expect with Lacey as I made sure the kids were buckled in before smiling at my mom in the passenger seat as I flew out of the driveway and made my way to the hospital as if our lives depended on it. These past few weeks had been devastating and heart-wrenching on all of us, so maybe our lives did depend on it. Maybe we all needed to see her and know she was okay so we could start to feel okay again ourselves.

A few minutes later the truck slid into a parking space and everyone climbed out, excitement radiating off of all of us. I prayed that Lacey was going to be the same as she was before the attack but I had to prepare myself that she might not be. I had vivid flashbacks of coming to this very hospital to see Renee, expecting to see the woman I knew and loved, but instead, I saw the shell of that woman as cancer ate away at every tiny bit of her that was left. I pushed the thoughts out of my head as I headed for the receptionist's desk and asked what room Lacey was in.

The long hallway through the ICU was empty and eerily quiet as we walked quickly to the room number the nurse had given me. I knocked gently on the door before opening it and stepping inside. I held my hand back and asked the kids to stay put for a second so I could make sure it was okay for them to go in. I had no idea what to expect since she was still in the ICU and wanted to be prepared before the kids were possibly blindsided. I walked a few steps in and gently pulled the curtain to the side to find Lacey leaning back against the pillow with her eyes closed. She looked beautiful, even with the faded bruises on her face and the ones on her neck that made my stomach knot. I took a few more steps toward her, trying to be quiet as I debated whether we should let her rest and come back later.

Her eyes fluttered open and her face lit up as she saw me. She struggled to push herself up into a seated position as I rushed over to help her.

"You're here," she whispered happily, looking up at me as if I were a figment of her imagination. I gently reached over and brushed my thumb against her cheek.

"There's nowhere else in the world I would rather be," I said as I smiled down at her. "I have someone else who is dying to see you."

I planted a quick kiss on her forehead before scurrying off to get my mom and the kids. I pulled the curtain back and stood to the side before I opened the door and waited for Annie to come in. I could hear Liam and my mom coaxing her to go in, my heart breaking for her knowing how scared she was of what she would find on the other side. A few seconds later, her head popped in around the corner and her eyes went wide when she saw Lacey.

"Mommy!!" she cried as she ran across the room and went to the side of the bed where Lacey was reaching over, arms wide open as she waited to hug Annie. I wiped a tear away as I saw them hold each other, Lacey's own rushing down her face as she held her daughter as tight as she could.

"I was so scared, mommy, I didn't want to lose you," Annie cried as she held onto Lacey.

I wrapped an arm around Liam's shoulders as we stayed off to the side with my mom, giving the girls some time together.

"I know, princess, I'm so sorry you had to go through that. But I'm okay, baby." Lacey rubbed her hand up and down Annie's back, pulling the IV in her hand in the process. I saw the moment she flinched as it pulled against the tape and remembered that we still didn't know how Lacey was feeling. Having been in a coma for two weeks, there were a lot of unknowns that the doctors had been waiting on before they could confirm if she would be able to go back to her normal self. Who knew what normal would be at this point?

Annie pulled back and sat on the edge of Lacey's bed, clutching her stuffed puppy to her chest.

"I tried not to be scared, but then daddy came to visit me in a dream, and he told me that you had talked to him recently and you were mad at him. He didn't know if you were going to have to stay in heaven with him, but he wanted me to know that he would still watch over me. So I felt better knowing that I had both Daddy and Grant, to watch over me. I really missed you though."

Lacey's face fell as she listened to Annie and I wondered if it had upset her to hear about Annie's dream. I had known about it from when she first told me the next morning, but maybe it bothered Lacey because it was her ex-husband and she knew how hard it was for Annie to lose her father.

"Did daddy say anything else to you in the dream?" she asked quietly.

"He mentioned that you were going to be looking for something and that was it. It didn't really make sense," Annie shrugged and Lacey nodded before glancing up at me.

"Hey, Liam," Lacey said with a smile as she looked down and caught his eye. I patted his shoulder and smiled when he rushed over to go see Lacey. Annie scooted over on the bed and left a space for Liam to reach up and get a hug from Lacey. It warmed my heart to see how much they loved each other. My mom sniffled next to me as she tried to wipe her tears away with the back of her hand. I reached over and wrapped my arm around her, pulling her in for a hug as I said a quick thank you that we were all in this room together, crying tears of happiness.

A little while later my mom had taken the kids down to the cafeteria for ice cream to give Lacey and me some time to talk. I had offered to go and let her get some rest but she quickly rejected that idea and told me that she didn't want to be away from any of us, ever again. She leaned against the pillows that I had fluffed and tucked behind her as I went over everything that had happened. She had a few questions but overall she seemed to be taking everything in and processing it.

I watched as the tears filled her eyes when I told her about Wyatt and smiled when she laughed after I told her that he hit on every nurse who tried to take care of him that they eventually had to rotate in all of the male nurses until he was discharged. We talked about her father and the complications during surgery but I had a hard time figuring out how she felt about the news that he had died. She sucked in a deep breath and held it as I talked, slowly blowing it out when I told her that the police would be in touch with her soon to discuss the next steps.

"So, did the house burn completely down?" she asked quietly as her fingers ran along the vein in my hand as I cuddled up next to her in the hospital bed.

"It's not *completely* down, but it's not safe to enter at this point. There's no telling when the rest of it will collapse."

"Grant, I am so sorry," she sighed heavily and looked up at me. "I am responsible for all of this and I feel terrible about it! I got your brother stabbed, your house burned down—literally everything is my fault."

She dropped her head and looked down in shame before I gently pressed my finger under her chin and lifted it.

"Lacey, none of this was your fault. You can't take the blame for anything that happened. And everyone is okay, you're safe, and you never have to live in fear of your dad again." I smiled and watched as her face changed like she was trying to recall something.

"What is it?" I asked, pulling to the side to see her better.

"Nothing," she said, still lost in thought. A few seconds later she turned to look at me and asked, "Did my dad die right away?"

I paused for a minute before answering her, wondering why she was asking. But if it helped her to move on by knowing all of the details, I didn't see what it would hurt to give them to her.

"No, he didn't die right away. He was actually in recovery, then had some complications and was rushed back to surgery. That was when he passed."

"Where was I when it was happening?"

"Um, gosh, I don't know," I drug a hand through my hair as I tried to remember the timeline of everything that had happened over the past few weeks. "Let me think about it for a minute."

I closed my eyes and tried to remember the details of everything then suddenly it came rushing back to me.

"You were in surgery and they were having a hard time stabilizing you. I know for a fact because I remember begging God to spare your life and let you live. I asked if he had to take one, that he make the right choice and take the one who didn't deserve to be here anymore."

Her shoulders fell and she looked away from me.

"Why do you ask?" I pushed, hoping to get her talking about whatever was weighing on her mind.

"It's nothing, it's silly more than anything," she paused and looked at me, unsure of whether to tell me. "I had this crazy, intense dream that I got to talk to Derek and my mom. She asked what I wanted and I told her that I wanted my family—you, Annie, and Liam and that I didn't want to live in fear of my father anymore. Next thing I knew she was shoving me in my chest and shouting clear as the dream ended."

I felt a chill run up my spine and tried to shake it off.

"Maybe it wasn't a dream, maybe it was you getting a chance to talk to her?"

"Maybe," she shrugged. "I talked to Derek as well, and if it wasn't a dream, then I saw how he died and everything that led up to it."

"You mean the accident?" I asked as I pulled her closer to me when I saw her shiver.

"Yeah, except in my dream, it wasn't an accident. He purposely crashed his car and killed himself so Annie and I would be taken care of with the insurance policy he had."

"That's intense," I whispered, running my hand up and down her arm as she laid her head on my chest and talked.

"Very." She let out a heavy sigh and sunk deeper into my side.

"But if it wasn't just a dream, if it was real—then I have to accept the fact that my husband didn't die on accident. He told me in my dream that he was drowning and that everything was about to go under. We were going to lose the house, he was going to lose his business—there wasn't anything he could other than kill himself to set us free. I could feel his pain and truly saw it in my dream which is a total mind game compared to how I remember him before he died. How am I supposed to know what the truth is? How will I ever know whether my husband died by accident or if he purposely killed himself to try to protect me and Annie?" Her voice started to rise as panic started to take hold.

"I don't know that there ever will be a way to know what the truth is," I offered as I looked down at her and met her gaze. "But if he did do it to make sure that you guys would be taken care of with the life insurance policy, then I guess you have to see that as being pretty selfless and brave. To love someone so much that you would make the ultimate sacrifice to make sure they were okay, that's a lot of love, Lacey."

"But there wasn't a life insurance policy, or at least if there was, I know nothing about it."

"Is there someone you can ask about it? Like whoever handled his estate?" I asked, remembering how overwhelming everything had been when Renee died, even after we had purposely taken the time to set everything up to make it easier.

"His brother was supposed to handle everything but I couldn't deal with it when it happened so I asked him to just do what he needed to and didn't ask any questions. He mentioned that he needed our bank account number, but I just figured it was so he could pay for expenses, like the burial."

"Have you checked that bank account, Lacey?" I asked softly, watching as it hit her. She brought a hand to her mouth and covered it as she shook her head.

"No, I haven't. Honestly, I didn't think much about it because I knew the balance in our account was high from selling the house so I didn't have to bother with logging in to check the account." She turned to look up at me, tears in her eyes again. "I'm so stupid, I should have checked and I shouldn't have ignored all of the phone calls from his brother after the funeral. I was in so much pain that I couldn't talk to any of his family, it was just too much at the time."

"Well, once we get you home, we'll check on everything and I can help you get in touch with his brother to make sure everything is wrapped up."

"Where is home?" she asked as she turned her head up to look at me.

"Right now, the kids and I have been living with my mother. But now that you're back, I wanted to talk to you about what you would like to do—assuming we are past the phase of you still trying to sneak out and book a hotel?" I teased as she blushed and giggled.

"We can either buy a new house once the insurance wraps up the claim or we can build a house together. Something that we both want, something for *our* family."

She lifted her finger to her mouth and tapped it a few times as she thought about it.

"I think I want to build a house with you, Mr. Walker. Something big and beautiful for our perfectly blended family."

She lightly reached up and pressed her lips to mine, offering me the sweetest kiss that I've ever had.

198

<u>Epilogue</u>
Grant- Eight Months Later

"Don't just sit there, rip them open!" I taunted as the kids sat in front of the Christmas tree in their matching pajamas. Lacey had picked out matching family pajamas for us to wear as a family for our first Christmas together in our new house. She was curled up in my lap as we rocked gently in my chair, watching the kids look at their presents as they decided which to open first.

We had decided to live with my mom while we knocked down the old house and built a brand new one. Everyone had a say in what they wanted with the new house and we tried to make sure we could accommodate all of them. Annie had wanted room in the backyard for a swing set and Liam had wanted a treehouse, which was rather impossible given that there were no trees in the backyard. So we compromised and got a giant swing set that came with a built-in treehouse that seemed to please everyone for the time being.

Lacey had asked for an oversized tub and larger master bathroom than we had before, which was fine by me as long as she agreed to part with those god-awful face masks. She wiggled her feet with excitement as Liam opened a gift from her and I rolled my eyes at the socks she was wearing, red with a giant cartoon penguin right smack in the center of her foot. I wanted to build a shop in the back, a place that I could work on projects and build things but after we added in the stuff for the kids, there wasn't much room back there for an additional structure.

As the contractors were building the house, I had come by to check in and see how things were going when I realized there was a huge mistake in the framing they had done compared to the blueprints we had given them. Everything else was perfect with a large kitchen and dining room area downstairs with an open concept that flowed into the living room so Lacey could keep an eye on the kids while she was cooking. Down the hall toward the extra bathroom, there was an additional room that we hadn't talked about.

I asked to see the blueprints and was surprised when they handed me a copy I hadn't seen before. At the back of the house, where we had agreed everything would end, was a new room that Lacey had added and labeled "man cave". The room spread the entire length of the house and was larger than I had talked about with my original idea. The room was separated into smaller spaces including a home theater that we could all enjoy on our weekly movie night, as well as a separate office that was just mine.

I had rushed back to my mom's house and pulled Lacey to the side, asking if she knew about the new plans. Which in hindsight was rather stupid, given that she was the one who had given them to the contractor to replace the original one. She smiled warmly as she heard the excitement in my voice, my mind still completely blown that she would do such a thoughtful thing for me.

The additional room had been way out of budget, but then I found that there were other amenities that we had decided to skip because of cost, that Lacey had gone back and added in without telling me. My heart was bursting at the seam as I realized how much she wanted to give us everything we had ever wanted in our house. While I tried to be logical and rational, she thought it was time to live a little on the wild side and splurge a little.

After she was discharged we had looked at her bank accounts and spoke to Derek's brother who had confirmed that he did have a life insurance policy in place but that he hadn't been able to file a claim until Lacey was ready because they required her signature. The process was rather quick after that and Lacey felt oddly at peace with everything she had learned from his brother who had to handle things after he passed. It seemed no one really knew the real Derek until after he was gone. Maybe that was true about all of us?

Lacey had put the bulk of the money into savings and used some of it to pay for the extra things she wanted for the house, as well as buying new furniture. The kids enjoyed their quick shopping spree as they picked out stuff for their own bedrooms, no longer having to share one. Lacey had insisted on an extra bedroom which seemed odd given she had given me an office downstairs as well as the massive backyard set up for the kids. When I asked her about it, she simply said, "you never know when we might need it."

The kids continued to shriek as they opened their presents, excitement filling the room and making my heart full and happy. I had already talked to the kids about it and they knew my plan but my palms started to sweat as I patted my pocket of my joggers to make sure the ring was still there. Liam looked up at me and raised his eyebrows, looking for the clue that we had agreed would be the signal that I was about to do it. I winked and his face lit up as he looked over at Annie and winked. Lacey smiled and looked between the kids, curious about their sudden odd behavior. She turned to look at me with a puzzled expression on her face before Liam called her name and pulled her attention away from me.

"Lacey, can you come help me open this? I really want to check it out," Liam said, looking past her as he made eye contact with me and attempted another wink. I chuckled as I watched how terrible he was with being subtle as Lacey climbed off my lap and glanced back at me.

"Sure, kiddo, what do you got?"

I waited until she was bent over by Liam, looking down at whatever random toy he was pretending to need help with. I sucked in a deep breath and pulled the ring out of my pocket, smiling at Annie as she watched, her face lit up with a huge smile. I dropped down to one knee and waited for Lacey to turn around.

"Never mind, I think I got it," Liam said with another wink to me.

Lacey stood up and put her hands on her hips as she looked between the kids.

"Okay, what's going on?" she asked before she turned around and spotted me. A small gasp escaped her throat as she clutched a hand to her chest. "Grant?" her voice trailed off.

"Lacey, I have loved you through so much already that I can't imagine spending a single minute apart from you. I want to spend the rest of our lives together, eating fried chicken and playing Monopoly, as we grow old together and watch our children grow up. Will you do me the honor of being my wife?" I held up the ring and watched the tears roll down her face as a faint blush flushed her cheeks, knowing she knew damn well what I was talking about with fried chicken and Monopoly.

"Yes!" she cried and gave me her hand. Mine slightly trembled as she watched me slide the ring onto her finger. I quickly stood up and wrapped her in my arms, swinging her around as she giggled and held onto me.

Thirty minutes later we had all finished opening our presents from each other as we sat in a giant pile of torn-up wrapping paper. I pulled Lacey over to me and wrapped my arm around her as I looked at the beautiful children we now shared.

"Did everyone get what they wanted for Christmas?" I asked, watching their angelic faces in the glow of the lights from the tree.

"Yeah, thank you guys so much, I can't wait to start playing with all of this," Liam said excitedly. Annie looked down at the worn-out puppy in her lap and nervously played with its ear.

"Annie, was there something you wanted for Christmas that you didn't get?" I asked gently, trying to think back to the list that Lacey and I had worked off together when we did our shopping. If there was something she wanted that she didn't get, it must not have been on the list she had given to us to give to Santa. Lacey tilted her head and waited for Annie to answer.

"No, I got everything I asked for," she said with disappointment heavy in her voice.

"But was there something that you *wanted* that you didn't get?" Lacey coaxed, pulling Annie's attention over to her as her lower lip trembled as she tried to hold back the tears.

"I asked Santa for something special when I saw him at the store. He said he would do his best to make it happen but I guess he just wasn't able to."

"What did you ask for?" Lacey and I asked at the same time, then laughed. Annie looked down then glanced over at Liam.

"It's okay, you should tell them," he said quietly and I immediately wondered what secret they were sharing and what she could possibly want that meant this much to her.

"I asked Santa for a baby," she whispered.

Lacey's head pulled back in confusion as I leaned forward to try to hear her better.

"Like a baby doll?" Lacey asked.

"No, like a real baby. I asked that Santa would bring me a new baby brother or sister," she sighed. "Well, technically, I asked him to bring one of each." She giggled and looked over at Liam as she brought the stuffed puppy up to her mouth to try to hide the smile.

"Honey, it doesn't really work that way," I started to explain. Lacey and I had talked about expanding our family several times and agreed that when the time was right, we would know it. There had been so much going on these past few months that it didn't seem like now would be the time to add to what we already had on our plate.

"I know, I'm sorry I asked," Annie apologized and looked down again. I looked over at Lacey, wondering what she wanted to do to try to make Annie feel better. We had been trying to work together as a team since we became an instant family but I was feeling completely lost on how to make a little girl feel better about Santa not granting her wish to have a real-life newborn sibling.

There was a calm look of peace on Lacie's face as she smiled sweetly at Annie before she turned to look at me and placed a hand on her stomach.

"Actually…" she said slowly as she caught my eye and looked deep into my eyes. "I have one more gift for you, but it's a little hard to unwrap…"

I nodded as I waited, unsure of what to think.

"I'm pregnant," she said cheerfully, a smile stretching across her face. "With twins."

I felt as if everything around me shifted at once as the kids got up and jumped up and down excitedly as they celebrated the news. I reached forward and grabbed Lacey, pulling her into me as I ran a hand along her stomach.

"I think that might be the best gift you could ever give me," I whispered in her ear as my heart burst with happiness.

204

Other Books By Samantha Baca

The Haven Brook Series:
'Til Death Do Us Part (Haven Brook Book 1)
https://books2read.com/u/m2RJNR

The Cradle Will Fall (Haven Brook Book 2)
https://books2read.com/u/b6O0QE

The Ties That Bind (Haven Brook Book 3)
https://books2read.com/u/mqgoz8

A Very Haven Christmas (Haven Brook Book 4- Novella)
https://books2read.com/u/mvqGjj

Three Strikes, You're Gone (Haven Brook Book 5)
https://books2read.com/u/mvqL2z

The Dark Shadows Series
Five Steps Ahead (Dark Shadows Book 1)
https://books2read.com/u/38Q0gO

Ten Seconds Too Late (Dark Shadows Book 2)
Coming 2022

Against The Clock (Dark Shadows Book 3)
Coming 2022

Out Of Time (Dark Shadows Book 4)
Coming 2023

<u>The Stone Creek Series (Novellas)</u>
Chocolate Covered Mistletoe (Stone Creek Book 1)
https://books2read.com/u/3LRk9N

Candy Coated Promises (Stone Creek Book 2)
https://books2read.com/u/mldP5Y

Pumpkin Spiced Possibilities (Stone Creek Book 3)
https://books2read.com/u/bojdwV

<u>Stand-Alone Books</u>
One Last Wish
https://books2read.com/u/mqg7D9

Finding Love In Apartment 2C (Novella)
https://books2read.com/u/bze9aZ

Acknowledgments

As always, thank you to all of the readers for picking up a copy of my book. I appreciate each and every one of you and hope you enjoy the stories that I write.

Thank you to my amazing supporters- my family and friends. I appreciate all of you sharing my posts and telling your friends and family about my books. I still get excited when I get a text message about how much you loved the book, and better yet, when I get a text message with you cursing me out for something one of the characters did.

Azucena, thank you so much for being such a constant force in my writing. I love that we can always bounce ideas off of each other and that you offer support in all aspects of my life, not just my writing. You are so valuable and I don't know what I would do without you. So don't ever leave me, okay?!

Chelsea, our friendship has changed so much this year and I'm so thankful that you're in my life and that I have you to help me with each book. I love talking with you about the books and working through plot twists as we plan things out. You've been a wonderful friend and an amazing alpha reader. Thank you so much for everything, and promise you won't leave me either...

Tillie, I still giggle when I read through your edits with the comments you leave with your reactions to the book. Those are my absolute favorite! I love that you jump in so quickly to read the books for me and that you give me feedback along the way so I make the book that much better. You're such a wonderful friend and I really appreciate all of your help!

Amanda, thank you for being so eager to read this book and for helping me with edits as well as pulling out some great teasers! You're always so supportive and I really love the friendship that we've developed along the way.

Debi, I love how quickly you read each book while also taking the time to proofread for me. Thank you for loving my books so much that you're excited to read the next one. I adore our relationship and couldn't imagine a world where we didn't support each other.

I always hold a special place in my heart for my parents and sister who support me with every single book and are always so eager to tell people they know about them. Thank you for always being my loudest cheerleaders and for constantly believing in me. I love you guys!

To my sweet husband, thank you for always being my superhero. I've said it before, and I'll say it again— thank you for moving Heaven and Earth to make things happen for me. I know it's not always easy to get everything done and I appreciate you making the time and putting in the effort for me. I love you and am so thankful to have you in my life.

To my sweet girls- as always, keep reaching for your dreams and enjoy the sweet moments when you watch them come true.

About the Author

Samantha lives in the southwest with her husband and two small children after abandoning her childhood dream of living in a cabin in Colorado when she found that she couldn't afford to live there and was deathly allergic to the woods. When she's not writing she's usually spouting off sarcastic remarks while drinking wine out of a coffee mug to look like a functional adult while chasing down her toddlers. She enjoys spending time with her family, watching reruns of FRIENDS, and the 24/7 flow of coffee that can be found in her veins. Be sure to follow her on social media for updates on what she's working on.

You can find her here:

Facebook: https://www.facebook.com/AuthorSamanthaBaca

Instagram: https://instagram.com/author_samantha_baca

Goodreads: http://www.goodreads.com/authorsamanthabaca

Facebook Reader Group:
https://www.facebook.com/groups/2945710968775398/

Webpage: https://authorsamanthabaca.wordpress.com

Newsletter: http://eepurl.com/g0NcSj